Balancing the Scales

The Twenty-Sided Sorceress: Book Ten

Annie Bellet

Copyright 2020, Annie Bellet and AnneMarie Buhl

All rights reserved. Published by Doomed Muse Press.

This novel is a work of fiction. All characters, places, and incidents described in this publication are used fictitiously, or are entirely fictional.

No part of this publication may be reproduced or transmitted, in any form or by any means, except by an authorized retailer, or with written permission of the publisher. Inquiries may be addressed via email to doomedmuse.press@gmail.com.

Cover designed by Ravven (www.ravven.com)
Formatting by Polgarus Studio (www.polgarusstudio.com)

If you want to be notified when Annie Bellet's next novel is released and get free stories and occasional other goodies, please sign up for her mailing list by going to: http://tinyurl.com/anniebellet Your email address will never be shared and you can unsubscribe at any time.

This book is dedicated to Una.
She was the first to tell me it was okay to make things up.
Go raibh míle maith agat.

Harper

Harper waved at the retreating backs of Softpaw's pack as they disappeared into the trees. The wolves were heading to the Den to report on the fight and its outcome with the sorcerer in the Frank to Freyda. Harper squinted toward the buildings on the edge of Wylde, debating if she could get away with being a fox to make the run ahead easier. With a heavy sigh she decided it was too far into daylight to risk. Too many potential humans around on this bright summer morning. Her clothes weren't the cleanest after she'd helped the pack get rid of bodies half the night, but while she could still faintly smell blood, she couldn't see too many obvious stains.

The day after a huge fight was always strange. Her world had shattered when she thought Jade was lost under a ton of rock and dirt, and then rebuilt itself again when they finally defeated the evil sorcerer who was severing shifters from their animal halves. The aftermath was burying bodies followed by a quick sleep on the forest floor. Harper knew she hadn't processed what had happened yet. Or perhaps she was growing used to this. *Oh, another evil bastard showing up needing a kick in the ass? No problem. 'Round these parts we call this "Tuesday."*

Harper swallowed a giggle. Yeah, she was definitely short on sleep and maybe sanity. She squared her shoulders and took off at a jog. She needed to go see Jade, make sure her friend was all right. She'd looked pretty smashed but she had Alek to watch over her. Odds were Jade was still sleeping off the big magics. Harper figured she had time to grab some food. Or maybe a shower first. Harper sniffed her shoulder and nodded. Definitely shower before food.

Harper pulled her phone out and turned it on as she climbed the steps to her apartment. There was one text from Ezee asking if things were good and if they were coming back yet. Harper sent a smiley face and a thumb's up. Then she added "back from honeymoon?"

"Had a weird feeling." Her phone buzzed almost immediately. "Also mosquitoes."

"Sounds like paradise," she texted back, adding a few flower emojis. Part of her wished that Ezee and Iollan had stayed away, stayed in their happy newlywed bubble a little longer. She imagined that Levi had filled in his twin and the druid on the new shitstorms circling Wylde by now.

"Paradise for mosquitoes. Where are you? Safe?"

"Totes safe. At apartment. Heading to Pwned after shower."

"Meet you there."

Jade, or more likely Alek since Harper would bet Jade hadn't been awake when they arrived, would have explained most of it, but it felt weirdly good that her friends were worried about her, too. She'd learned the hard way that pulling away from people after stressful situations or times of danger ultimately made the trauma worse. It was good to have people and she had the best people. Even if she was a terrible friend for being glad her newly-wedded bestie was home to fight whatever ugly came next. Facing down evil just wasn't the same without friends.

An hour later, showered, changed into clothes that hadn't been within two feet of multiple dead bodies, and with a Hot Pocket making a lump in her stomach, Harper pushed through the door of Pwned Comics and Games. Lara looked up from behind the counter and the relief in her brown eyes was obvious even from the doorway. Levi and Ezee leapt up from where they'd been lounging in the big chairs Jade had installed toward the back by the new release racks. Concern lined Ezee's handsome face and Harper swore she saw at least two wrinkles in his normally impeccable button-down shirt. Levi was chewing on one of his lip piercings and his mohawk looked as though he'd been running nervous fingers through it all night. His teeshirt was rumpled as well. He had to have been worried if he'd left Junebug's side at the Den.

All three of her friends looked past Harper as though they expected someone to come in behind. It was obvious enough that she paused and looked over her shoulder, even though with her keen senses she knew nobody was there. What the hell was going on?

Then she looked around again, peering past the twins. No Jade. No Alek. Harper hoped Jade was still asleep and Alek was upstairs watching over her.

Sometimes Jade slept for a day or more after draining her magic reserves. But Harper's friends looked as though they'd been keeping a damn vigil all night and their concerned faces scared her. It was so at odds with the joking demeanor of Ezee's texts. Harper tried to shove away the hot thread of worry that wrapped itself around her throat.

"Where are Jade and Alek?" Ezee said, and the thread turned into a noose.

"What do you mean where are Jade and Alek?" Harper said, searching their faces. "They left last night, should have been back late. Did you knock upstairs?"

"Nobody is in, we're sure of it. Jade and Alek aren't answering their phones, either," Levi said.

"Why didn't you say that before?" Harper waved her phone at them. There had to be a good, reasonable explanation for why Jade and Alek were out of contact. Maybe nobody had knocked loud enough. That had to be it.

"We figured they were right behind you, and you sounded fine, so I guess we assumed everything was fine?" Ezee said.

"Everything *was* fine."

Harper pushed past them and made her way to the

back of the shop. She unlocked the rear door and leaned out, looking around the parking lot. No truck. Jade's car was there but the truck they'd borrowed from the logging camp the night before, the truck that Jade and Alek should have arrived home safe and sound in, it wasn't there. A million justifications started piling up in Harper's mind as she stalked back down the hall to her friends.

"We defeated the sorcerer," she said. "Jade was how she gets after a big fight, especially cause she got a mountain dropped on her at one point, but Alek was driving. I mean…" Harper paused to take a breath, feeling the weight of everyone's worried gazes on her. "We won. Everything was fine."

"Maybe they hit another moose," Levi said with a forced smile that was more grimace than grin.

Lara shook her head. "I can try calling her phone again?"

"What if Bob got her?" Levi said, jumping straight to what everyone was thinking.

"Bob?" Harper said, even though she had a feeling who he meant.

"Yeah, we decided the First needed a name. Bob. Big Old Bad."

"You decided," Ezee muttered. "Besides, his name is probably the old timey European equivalent of 'John'."

"I think John *is* the old timey European equivalent of John," Lara said.

"Johnbob?" Levi's smile was almost convincing this time.

"No." Ezee glared at his twin.

"We don't have to assume the worst. Shit happens. They were tired, it was a long day. Maybe they stopped somewhere to rest?" Harper said. She stepped between the twins, hands up in a placating gesture.

Levi and Ezee both gave her flat, disbelieving looks but that was the best explanation she could come up with that didn't involve Bob. All the others ranged from bad to really fucking bad. Sure, the First was still out there and who knew what minions of evil he had running around but not everything had to be terrible all the time.

Maybe. Probably. And yet Jade had been so tired, so weak, and while she was immortal, Alek wasn't, and the First definitely had it out for the former Justice.

"She had her phone, yeah?" Lara tapped her fingers on the counter, drawing Harper's attention back to reality.

"Yeah, pretty sure."

"It's ringing before going to voicemail, so I think it isn't shut off. Hang on." Lara went to the main computer and pulled up a search page.

"You are searching 'where's my phone?'" Ezee asked as he crowded up beside Harper at the counter.

"Jade leaves her email logged-in on like everything," Lara said.

"There!" Harper pointed and then put her hand down, feeling like a dork. On the map a dot had popped up, showing Jade's phone's location.

In the middle of nowhere, Idaho. Well, not quite nowhere.

"Zoom out a bit," Harper said.

Lara complied.

"There, that road, that's what they would have hit after leaving the woods. See? It connects up with the highway into Wylde there." She wished she had a laser pointer but stabbing her finger at the screen seemed to get the point across. "So Jade's phone is kind of along the route they would have taken."

"But why there? There's no *there* there." Levi leaned over the counter for a better look.

Lara zoomed way in and set the map to satellite

view. There was the road and the bumpy hills of the Frank.

"So something happened. Maybe there's a cabin or something we can't see. A quaint little B&B?" Harper was still reaching for optimistic straws. Her breakfast was a greasy lump in her belly and her heart raced like it could somehow catch up to a version of reality that didn't suck if it just beat fast enough.

"Maybe," Levi said but he was already reaching for his keys.

"I'll stay, keep the place open, and call you just in case they show up, cool?" Lara said.

"Send the coordinates to me," Ezee said, following Levi toward the back of the store.

"You gonna be okay?" Harper said, realizing they were all leaving Lara alone in the store.

"Harper, go," Lara squeezed Harper's hand quickly. "Go get our girl."

"She's probably fine. She's like immortal and shit." The words felt weird in her mouth, as though even her own tongue was aware how thin and hollow the sentiment was. How unlikely.

"It's gonna be fine," Harper said as she climbed into Levi's car.

Levi drove like the world was cop-free, speeding tickets were for other people, and his tires were aflame. It still took an hour to get to the turn-off from the main highway and another silent, tense fifteen minutes to find the coordinates.

Levi slowed finally as they approached where the phone should be. Nothing. They crept along, nobody speaking. Harper rolled down her window and Ezee and Levi followed her lead.

"Smell that?" Harper said, her heart trying to kick out of her chest again.

"Like Fourth of July," Levi muttered.

"Shit," Ezee said as Harper's gaze fell on the swath of ripped up vegetation to the side of the road ahead.

The road climbed a small hill here and the brush to either side was thick with summer green and growth. A large section had been torn up on the downhill side as though something huge had smashed right through.

Something like a truck.

Levi pulled over onto the uphill side across from the torn-up section. The smell of gunpowder was there, but faded, as though it had been hours since whatever caused it had gone off.

Harper forced her fists to uncurl as she looked

around. "Tire marks," she said, pointing to the ground near where they'd parked.

"Someone accelerated hard here—see how the dirt is kicked up?" Levi bent and touched the furrows.

"Like they were going straight at the road," Harper said, turning and looking across to where the broken branches and smashed leaves lay open like a gash.

Without speaking, the three of them picked their way across the road and started down the hill.

"No, fuck no," Harper sobbed as she accelerated, more sliding than running down the hill. "That's the truck."

The sickly sweet scent of blood, too much blood, vied with the strengthening scent of gunpowder. The land flattened almost immediately and there, in a heap of bullet-scored metal and broken glass, lay the truck that Alek had been driving. A long smear of semi-dried blood buzzing with flies stained the ground brown and black and greasy. The truck had flipped and gone upside down, the passenger side crumpled almost completely in by outside force.

There were no bodies, but a dozen or more boot prints in the dry dirt told a story along with the hundreds of spent shell casings.

"No bodies," Levi said, echoing Harper's desperate thoughts.

"Jade's phone," Ezee said as he ducked into the half-collapsed truck cab and fished it out of a pile of blood-smeared glass. "Still on."

"What is, oh," Harper started to say as a clump of stringy black hair and greyish goo slid off the phone and hit the ground with a splat. Her Hot Pocket came up in a lump as she stumbled away to vomit.

"Is that Jade's hair?" Levi asked even as he shook his head, denying the obvious. "But, no. Look, no bodies. We can solve this. We can fix this."

Harper wiped her mouth with her teeshirt and forced herself to turn back to the carnage. Levi's fists were clenched as though he could fight time itself to change the past. Ezee stood by the truck, still holding Jade's phone as though it were a puzzle he could solve. They both looked at her with dark, despairing eyes. There were no dice here to reroll. No books with answers. Just the wind muttering in the trees and flies buzzing over too-large bloodstains.

We've survived worse, Harper told herself. *We can do this.*

"Right. No bodies, okay?" She licked her lips and regretted it immediately as the taste of vomit mixed with the smell of blood and gunpowder.

"They might be hiding somewhere in the woods, licking wounds, something." Levi spun in a slow circle, nostrils flared.

"I'll call my husband," Ezee said. "This is wilderness enough that he could help."

Harper rubbed her palms on her jeans. "Okay. And we gotta call the sheriff. They'll have forensics. Let's not touch anything else. We know smart people who can solve this with us. Together."

But even as she said that, a silver glint inside the truck caught her eye. For a moment she thought it was just more windshield or window glass, but then the all-too-familiar shape compelled her forward. Crouching, Harper gingerly reached into the blood-stained shards and pulled out Jade's necklace.

Jade's D20 talisman. Hanging from its broken chain.

Harper stopped breathing. The buzzing of flies faded. It was as though the world held its breath with her as she turned the talisman to the one spot.

The divot that had held Samir's heart was empty.

"I hate to alarm y'all," Harper released the words in a gasp as her heart started beating again, "but we're super fucked."

1

Ice rimed the picnic table beneath me as I paused to perch there and watch half-frozen surfers catching waves on Lake Michigan. One had to admire their dedication, I supposed. From this distance they were gliding black shapes in the late afternoon sunlight. There were chunks of ice among the rocks on the shore as well, but the last snowfall had mostly melted away. It was cold and clear and my head felt like an axe had split it open. The waves were bottle brown turning to glassy green as they crested and caught the sun.

"There's a certain beauty in it, no?" Samir stepped up beside me and draped an arm around my shoulders.

"More like a certain crazy," I said, leaning into his

warmth. I tipped my head back to look up at him, confused for a moment why my brain had expected blue eyes instead of gold. Blond hair instead of black. I gave myself a mental shake. I'd woken up with a headache and it seemed to be getting worse, not better, despite the fresh air and exercise that Samir had promised would do me good.

"Still in a mood, I see." Samir chuckled.

I winced, for somehow the sound of his laugh made the headache worse. I pressed my fingertips to the bridge of my nose and was surprised to feel skin. I'd put on gloves before we went out, hadn't I? I stared at my hand as though it had done something offensive.

"Something is wrong," I said. Was this some kind of sorceress flu? I'd pushed my magic hard in our last couple training sessions though I couldn't quite remember why or what we had done. But my muscles were leaden and my magic… my magic… I tried to reach for it but only pain answered, like my blood was full of tiny razors. I stumbled to my feet, throwing off the weight of Samir's arm.

"Leave that alone, Jade," Samir said. His handsome face was stern and he reached for me again, his hands enclosing my upper arms. "You pushed too hard, you must rest."

I stared at his slender brown fingers. My mind was yelling that these were the wrong hands. That someone else was supposed to be here. It's Samir, I told myself. He's your boyfriend. You are in Michigan. You're a mage. Everything is fine. You're just tired.

I focused on the sensation of cold air on my face but even the chill was slipping away. I was too warm despite standing on the windy winter shore with only a sweater on.

"I put a coat on before we went out," I said. I had a distinct memory of that.

The little blue house with its wrap-around porch. Standing in the library complaining of a headache. Going out for a walk and pulling on my grey and blue wool coat. I looked down at myself. I was in a teeshirt. A teeshirt smeared with red liquid, the damp parts sticking to my skin. Now I felt the cold, but it was deep, the kind that starts in the bones, a freezing from the inside out.

Samir sighed. "Well, this is awkward." His smile wasn't friendly anymore but mocking. An expression I knew. A tone I was intimately familiar with.

I backed away from him. The blood on my shirt dried to black before my eyes. My mouth filled with metallic liquid and though I spat, nothing came out.

There was no sound of waves, I realized. No smell of the lake shore.

"This isn't real," I said aloud. I'd killed him. I remembered now though the image was alone without a lot of context. Samir kneeling in the snow. Wylde. My store, shelves full of comics and books and all the things that make me happy. People. Faces swam into my mind. Then names. Harper. Ezekiel. Levi.

Alek.

Alek. There was something I had to do, something I couldn't remember. But I was certain I had to save Alek.

"Oh, it is far too late for that," Samir said though I was sure I hadn't spoken aloud.

"I have to go. Let me go." I tried to reach for my magic again, to fling him away from me, to wake myself up from this nightmare. Pain was a cloak of biting insects swarming me, pulling me out of the dream and down, and away, and into the frozen dark.

My wrists were cuffed to something solid, perhaps a bed beneath me. I knew before I opened my eyes that the wrongness wasn't gone but at least this place had a smell. Stunk like a hospital, but that might have been from the industrial citrus-scented cleaning fluid scent filling the air.

It was not a hospital, at least not one I'd ever been in. I was indeed cuffed to a hospital-style bed by my wrists and ankles. There was no sheet on the bed beneath me, just a plastic covering. A thin white blanket covered my naked body. The room was a small concrete box with a single door. In the door was a smaller sliding metal window cover. A prison.

I'd gone to sleep in my bed and woken up in a horror movie. My eyes were crusted with gunk I tried to blink away and my head was still pounding as though it had been kicked in by something big and angry. I knew I had to be missing time, missing a key memory or two. Missing whatever the hell had happened to get me here.

"I'm sure it will come back to you now that you are awake," Samir said from behind me.

I twisted on the bed to try to see him. He sauntered around to the side, his lips twisted into a facsimile of a grin.

"You're not real," I said. He was dead. Well, mostly

dead. His heart was a tiny ruby in my talisman.

I jerked on the cuffs though it was pointless. I could see and feel the absence of my D20 talisman. Something jingled on my wrists as I moved them. There was another band of metal beneath the wide, padded cuffs.

"No, I'm not real anymore," Samir said with a shrug. "But this might be better. I can work with this."

Not words to comfort anyone. I fought the rising panic in my chest with a couple of deep breaths. There was no camera in the room that I could see but someone had locked me to this bed. They would have to come back. I tried to reach for my magic and hit a wall. Not razors of pain like in the dream, but a barrier, as though someone had put a cover on the pool. It was smooth like glass and I couldn't even begin to find a way through.

Not the end of the world, I reminded myself. I'd been without my magic before. This was a setback. I needed more information. I needed answers.

I needed to remember how I got here.

"Are you sure you want that?" Samir was still here and this time I was sure I hadn't spoken aloud.

"You are in my head," I said, glaring at him. Maybe

I was in this place because I'd suffered brain damage and now I was cursed to hallucinate my asshole ex for all eternity.

A memory tried to surface. Glass breaking. Loud cracks like fireworks going off but... no. Gunfire. I knew the difference.

"Let's go somewhere more interesting," Samir said. "No reason to jump straight to the climax without a little foreplay, no?"

"Get out. Get out." I gave into the panic, twisting and fighting with the thick leather and metal cuffs binding me. "Get out get out get out."

"On the contrary," he said, leaning over me until his face was all I could see. "Let's go in."

The bed and room were gone. I stood alone in a hallway full of doors. There were still cuffs on my wrists but they were more like silver bangles. I had clothes on again.

I knew this place. The hall was quiet, the world sleeping outside the dark windows. They were in the cafeteria and I had to get there. Even though it was impossible. Even though I knew there was no time. I had lived this nightmare a thousand times before.

I started running as the doors bowed with heat and

the walls crackled. That hadn't happened in real life but the memory didn't care. The first time, the real time, I'd been here with my hands full of light and power, screaming for my family, knowing Samir had them somewhere in the school.

"Jess! If you can hear me, run. There's no time," Ji-hoon's voice crackled over the PA system.

"It's a trap, Jess, go." Kayla's voice was too high and choked with anger and fear. Samir had left them with an open line, so I could hear them while I searched.

The chained doors of the cafeteria were ahead of me as I slid around a corner but no matter how fast I ran toward them they stayed the same distance away.

I couldn't reach them. I'd never reached them. I knew what was coming. The conversation was always the same, locked in my memory like a curse.

"If I tip this over, it'll go off." Todd's voice in the speakers.

"Set it off," Sophie said.

"She's right. If it goes off before Jess gets here, she'll be safe."

"We're setting off the bomb, Jess. Run. If you are here, turn around, run. Please." Ji-hoon's words echoed in the halls and in my memory.

"I love you guys," Sophie said.

"We love you, Jess," Kayla said with a sob. "I hope you can't hear us."

"I can hear you," I screamed even though they wouldn't hear me, they hadn't heard me then and this was only memory now. They would never hear me.

"Love you," Ji-hoon said.

"Love you all," Todd said.

The blast wave hit me first, the walls rippling as I was slammed off my feet. Then the heat. The fire alarms went off but not the sprinklers. Samir had seen to that. In that reality, Wolf had come and dragged me out. In this horrible nightmare memory, there was no Wolf, no one here for me at all. Just me screaming at the fire.

"That was fun," Samir said, crouching beside me. "Alas, you have a visitor. We will talk more later."

I was back on the bed in the cuffs with the white blanket twisting around my body as I struggled to free myself. Sobbing and screaming their names. Kayla. Ji-hoon. Todd. Sophie. A litany of grief and anger that quieted as the steel door opened. Through my tears I watched a slender white woman of middle years walk into the room. She wore her dark hair in a tight, smooth bun, carried a clipboard, and had a lab coat on.

She might have been a doctor or perhaps some kind of psychologist. I made myself breathe in a couple of deep, gulping breaths. I needed answers and I hoped she had them.

But I was sure of two things now.

First, that I had eaten Samir's heart.

And second, his mind-ghost was driving me insane.

2

Lab coat lady stopped a few feet away from the bed and made a show of checking her clipboard. She might as well have put a sign over her head in neon lights flashing "faking it" for how hard she was trying. It wasn't reassuring, given my magic-less state and the whole chained naked to a bed with no memory of how I got there situation. I knew I should let her say something first, see what line she took, but I couldn't do it. Not with Samir smirking at me.

"Who are you?" I said, going for the only obvious question that wouldn't give away how little I remembered about whatever had led to this predicament.

"Do you not remember?" lab coat lady asked. "You

were brought to us for treatment."

"She's lying," Samir said.

"Thanks, Captain Obvious," I muttered. Her eyebrows knit together and I raised my voice. "This isn't a hospital, so how about you try again?"

Lab coat lady's lips twisted in what she probably thought was a smile. "You don't remember how you got here, do you?" She sounded weirdly hopeful and it made my skin crawl.

"Where is here?" I asked. "Who are you?"

"You were in an accident," she said too quickly. "You were brought here to recover."

"She's a worse liar than you are," Samir said. He walked around behind the woman, a ghost in my mind made manifest, but clearly she had no idea he was there. I doubted he could affect the physical world; none of my other memory ghosts had. But he could be fucking annoying which was kinda the same thing.

I'd spent a quarter century, half my life really, letting Samir live rent-free in my head in a figurative way. I had no idea why I would have chosen to let him live there in a more concrete fashion.

"Let is a strong word," Samir said with a grin.

I flipped him the mental bird and tried again with lab coat lady.

"Look, we can go around in these circles all fucking day or night or whatever it is, or you can answer my questions. Or you can just unlock these cuffs, give me some fucking clothes, and I'll get out of your hair."

Whatever expression I made in lieu of a smile was clearly not pleasant from the way she took a large step back. After a deep breath she lowered her clipboard and gave herself a small shake.

"I am Special Agent Ainsley and I work for a branch of the US government," she said. "You are in possession of something that could be a threat to national security. You are being detained until its whereabouts are established and the artifact is secured."

Artifact? I tried to remember what I possibly had. Where I had been? What had I done last? My head started to ache again, images and bits of conversations with half-seen people flitting at the edges of my consciousness.

A memory swam into my head, fuzzy around the edges. Two men from the NoS, Not Otherwise Specified, division of Homeland Security or whatever department. They'd been asking about Samir. I'd lawyered up because I had something important to take care of.

Shifters.

Rockslide.

Like the tumble of stones and earth crashing down the hillside onto me, memories broke through. I gasped, hands clenching into fists. We'd been in the Frank, hunting another sorcerer who was severing shifters from their animal selves. A sorcerer named Ethan, who was after me.

"You? Truly?" Samir said in that same self-satisfied voice.

He was right. Not me. Ethan was after Samir's heart.

Like the old cliché of puzzle pieces sliding into place, the picture came together. Almost.

I still didn't know how I'd gotten here. I remembered being tired. Alek helping me into a truck.

Glass breaking.

Blood.

But the memory was gone before it formed as the woman stepped up to the bed.

"Do you remember?" she asked.

"You want the door?" I asked, recalling the door

that Samir had shipped to me which was, I hoped, still languishing in my back room.

"Door?" She shook her head. "Fine, I'll cut to it. We need Samir's heart, Ms. Crow."

"I am so very popular post-mortem," Samir said. "Pity you only have your heart to give them, now."

Ainsley didn't know that. Which was good. It meant the world hadn't ended yet, the supposed magic apocalypse that killing Samir good and proper dead would bring about.

"I suppose I failed to teach you that one should not believe everything one is told," Samir said. "The lies you were fed to get you to stop gaining additional power are staggering, truly."

"Can you shut up for even like half a second?" I asked him silently in my head. A wider grin was my only answer. He clearly had no intention of leaving me alone and I didn't know how to banish him without Wolf's help and Wolf was missing. Again.

Along with my memories of whatever happened after the fight with Ethan. I didn't believe in coincidences.

"Samir was vital to many of our operations," Ainsley said. "You must understand that the power in his heart cannot be unlocked. If it were to be consumed by a sorcerer or fall into the wrong hands, the consequences would be devastating."

I started to respond and then stopped. The government agents, whose names were lost to trauma and time—though I remembered the weird proto-porn-stache the older one had—hadn't known that Samir was dead-ish. But this lady was talking as though it was a known thing that I had killed him and that he was only mostly dead, with me continuing to hang on to his heart.

"Why do you think I have Samir's heart?" I said to buy time. I licked my cracked, chapped lips and struggled to get my sluggish brain to obey me.

Of the people who knew Samir wasn't truly dead, or at least hadn't been until recently, there were very few I didn't utterly trust. Mostly just the damned vampire Archivist. Would he have told the government? And if so, why not the agents who had shown up?

Except he'd clearly wanted Samir's heart for himself. The sorcerer Ethan was going to trade it for immortality for his lover.

"You are so close, it is fascinating how slowly your mind works," Samir said, moving to loom over the tense Agent Ainsley.

"And yet I'm not the dead guy," I told him.

His smirk didn't even crack for a second. As come backs go, it was not my finest work. Exhaustion hung on me heavier than the thin sheet and the manacles. I had to solve this and nobody here was helping. I wasn't going to fall for his gaslighting bullshit. If only Noah, the Archivist, had told me about the magical apocalypse, I would have been suspicious. But the first I'd heard of it was from my own father, who had saved my ass and as far as I could tell, hadn't lied to me about anything. Ash had been brutally honest from the get-go.

Same with Brie and Ciaran. They were my friends, but they also had knowledge and powers I didn't fully grasp. Brie being three goddesses sharing a skinsuit and Ciaran being a leprechaun. Brie had clearly wanted Samir *dead* dead, but knew the consequences of it and even warned me about them separately from Ash.

"Because gods and leprechauns never deceive humans for their own gain," Samir said. "I know you dropped out of college, but did you seriously not pay an ounce of attention to say, all of human literature and mythology?"

"Jade Crow?" Ainsley tapped her fingers on the rail

of my bed. "I need you to answer me. Where is Samir's heart? Tell me and we can discuss the terms of your release." Again she tried a smile but all I could see was Samir's condescending face hovering over her head.

"Here's my terms," I said, fighting the darkness creeping into my vision. "You release me, and I forget you exist."

"I had hoped you'd be more amenable and we could avoid harsher methods of interrogation," she said, backing away straight through Samir's smirking apparition. "I'll let you think about our offer. It is non-negotiable."

Before I could say anything else, she turned and practically fled the room. I saw nothing beyond the door but darkness.

"Damnit," I muttered.

I tried again to reach for my magic but the glass was still in place, locking me out. My body desperately wanted to sink into oblivion again, my very bones feeling like they'd gained a million pounds, my muscles weak and hardly tensing as I strained against the bindings. All I did was give myself a worse headache and bruise my wrists more. I couldn't even see a locking mechanism from the angle I could examine.

"You like the bracelets? I designed them myself."

"Of course you did." I gave up and lay back, fighting tears. Crying would just make me madder. And thirstier. Bitch hadn't even offered me water. "Where the hell did they get them? You handing out magical items to the government?"

Samir laughed, a cold, harsh sound in the empty room. "Hardly. If only you knew someone who loved to collect such items the mystery could be solved."

I forced myself to think, knowing Samir wouldn't give me a straight answer. He was having far too much fun tormenting me with my lack of memory. Ainsley, probably not her real name, was no NoS agent. She'd given away what they wanted too quickly and she'd been sure I had it. Which pointed to Noah, probably. So did the magic-nullifying bracelets under my cuffs. If anyone in the world could acquire items that powerful from Samir, it would be the Archivist. I could see the vampire wanting that kind of contingency plan if he had to subdue a sorcerer somehow.

Except there was a tiny problem with defaulting to Noah being my jailer. This whole scenario, right down to the comically bad Ainsley, had all the subtlety and finesse of a drunk sportsball fan in a china shop. It didn't feel like Noah's style. But perhaps whoever she really was, this woman had somehow bought the vital information from the vampire. Or was seeking it on his behalf, as Ethan had done.

My head hurt from trying to sort it out. Bits and parts of the last day of my life, or at least that I could remember as the last day, surfaced and faded in my mind. I pressed my wrists into the cold metal, seeking the pain to keep me awake. Sleep would mean less control over my mind. It would mean dreams.

"Sleep is so… healing." Samir leaned over me and I twisted my head to avoid his lips.

"You aren't real."

"I am real enough." Samir brushed hair back from my face. "I feel like myself, if a little disembodied." He chuckled at his own joke as he stroked my cheek.

"Fuck off. Or let me see what the hell happened to get me here." I snapped at his hand, but my teeth closed on air.

"I am not keeping that memory from you," he said. I felt his fingers in my hair, stroking through the tangles as though he was truly here. My scalp crawled. "That is all you, Jade. Perhaps you do not wish to remember."

"I should have let Alek eat you," I said. I whipped my head to the side too quickly and the room darkened, spinning.

Alek.

Breaking glass.

"Where is Alek?" I asked, my mind twisting away from the memory even as it started to solidify. "What the fuck did you do? What the fuck did I do?" My voice was a broken sob. I'd eaten Samir's heart.

The only way I could see me doing that was… I didn't know. I couldn't imagine. Except I could. Something horrible had to have happened.

"I guess it is time," Samir murmured over me, fisting my hair in his hands. "Remember?"

And I did. And I wished… I wished…. I could forget.

Harper

There were times, Harper reflected as she turned down the hallway toward the room she was sharing with her mother at the Den, that the last few weeks felt like a nightmare she could still wake up from. If she ignored the scents of dozens of strangers, she could almost imagine that the door she was opening led to her apartment, or perhaps to the game store. She would open it, Jade would be inside, and they would order pizza and plan the next game night.

Instead her room was cramped, two single beds shoved against the walls with a dresser between them. She'd had little time to grab things after the First's army came to Wylde. There was a picture of her, Max, and her mom. Her dice bag. Her mom's lotion bottle and a paperback romance novel with dog-eared pages.

Jade's D20 talisman on a new chain, laying there on the dresser like an offering. Or a warning. A grim reminder. There had been no news of Jade or Alek. Sheriff Lee had tried to investigate but before much could happen, she'd been put on leave. "Suggested vacation" as she put it. Someone higher up was pulling strings and Wylde was once again being abandoned by the human authorities. With two days of that shitty news, the first truckloads of hostile shifters started piling into town, rounding up shifter and human alike.

Harper, Rosie, the twins, Lara—they'd all made it out. Same with Vivian and Sheriff Lee. Others hadn't been so lucky. The Den now housed a couple hundred refugees. They used to come daily, but the flood of shifters looking for safety had slowed to a trickle. Then to a stop. Justice May had gone out days ago to contact a group and guide them here, but no word from her since had everyone even more on edge.

The First's army hadn't approached the Den yet. There'd been a few skirmishes as though they were testing defenses, but the First seemed content to secure Wylde itself. May and Freyda speculated that his mind-control abilities had limits and distance was one. But it left the shifters at the Den in a holding pattern, fortifying as best they could, and waiting with dread for more news, for any other survivors. Yosemite was doing what he could to help the land itself work in their favor, but the area around the Den wasn't quite wild enough for him to have easy control.

Harper had come to her room to get away from the noise in the Hall, to escape to the only quiet place left so that she could scream if she needed to without twenty people running to her rescue. Jade's talisman had been set down with the twenty showing upward, a gamer's prayer that something would start to go right. But for Harper, it only mocked her, hiding the empty divot where Samir's heart had been. Something terrible had happened and they would have to start facing the fact that war had come to Wylde and their champion was gone. She sat on the edge of her bed, weariness eating away her ability to fight the grief and despair.

"Ow!" Something hard poked her hip and she stood up quickly.

Laying on the bed was a sword, its battered leather sheath familiar to her.

Jade's sword. The Alpha and Omega. Last Harper had known, it was buried under a ton of rock and dirt. Harper stared at the blade, shaking her head slowly back and forth. She knew it was magical, that it showed up sometimes for Jade when she thought she'd lost it, but its presence here was just another sign that nothing was right in the world.

"Oh no, shoo. Go away. I do not want you. Go help Jade. Bring her back. Shoo."

The sword lay there. Because it was a sword. Harper laughed nervously to herself. Right.

"Okay, but you can't stay here." She gingerly picked it up, remembering how good it had felt the one time she used it. How easy it had been to kill the ghouls and zombies trying to take her down. This blade, which was two daggers magically joined somehow, could kill anything stone dead with just a nick, even undead. It was a killing machine.

Super dangerous. But perhaps also useful. The sword had come to her, so she'd at least offer it up as potentially helpful to the group. Just until Jade returned, of course. With a sigh, Harper carried it back to the hall.

The Great Hall at the Den was a meeting place with both a lower and upper gallery. It had been repurposed into a combination dining hall and crafting area. At one end of the hall, a platform had been built over the smooth bowl blasted into the stones by Jade when she'd swallowed a bomb with her magic a few years before. On the platform was a large table with stools around it where Freyda was overseeing the war effort, in a manner of speaking.

"Is that what I think it is?" Levi asked as Harper stepped up to the large table where he and some of the others were gathered around a map of Wylde which had too many red circles on it to make sense of at a glance.

"Isn't that Jade's?" Ezee said at the same time.

"It just showed up in my bed," Harper said. "Probably doesn't even work for me, anyone want it?"

"It chose you," Levi said.

"No it didn't—see?" Harper half drew the blade, which immediately began to glow blue.

"Yes, very convincing." Levi grinned, and Ezee gave Harper a helpless shrug as he waved a hand toward the blade.

"Calm your tits, Sting," Harper muttered as she shoved the sword back into its sheath. So much for being selfless and giving up the magic weapon.

"That sword, it can kill anything, yes? Even a sorcerer?" Freyda's eyes narrowed in speculation.

Harper glanced at the twins. She'd shared the information about how Jade had "defeated" Samir using the blade, essentially reducing him and his heart to a tiny gem, but in the ensuing chaos they had all decided that information should be need-to-know. Especially the part where Samir's heart was now missing along with Jade and Alek.

"It could at least fuck the First's day up," Harper said, edging around the answer.

"If you could get within striking distance without being mind-controlled or killed," Ezee said.

"That's a hell of an 'if,' though," Levi said.

Freyda sighed. "Still, it is something to think about. For later. Let's focus on what we can do now."

"What are we planning?" Harper asked.

"You're not going." Her mom, Rose, walked by the table carrying a full laundry basket.

Harper gave her mom a look and waited until she'd kept walking and her determined form was swallowed by the dozens of shifters eating and drinking and doing various tasks in the Great Hall.

"Medical supplies," Vivian said. "Rachel and I are

going to go raid my practice, provided it hasn't been already."

"Scouts reported that part of town was pretty bare of activity lately," Freyda said. The Alpha of Alphas had a pinched, tired expression.

"I should go, too—we need someone to look out for trouble while others get supplies," Ezee said, though his troubled face and tight shoulders said he didn't like the idea.

"No, you are newly married. Iollan would kill me," Rachel said. "We'll find another volunteer. Lots of folk here want something, anything to do."

"Lots of folk here don't know Wylde like we do," Ezee pointed out.

Harper looked at the sword in her hands. It felt like a sign, or maybe she wanted to get doing something, anything, to stop the endless cycle of wishing things would change. Of waiting for the damn hero to show up.

"I'm guess I'm your huckleberry," Harper said. "This stupid sword showed up for a reason, and it can kill anything, which means I'm the caravan guard."

"Oh no, your mom will kill me, and she's organized a veritable domestic army to keep this place running and everyone fed," Freyda said. "I'm not pissing her off."

"I've been pissing her off since before I was born," Harper said with a grin she almost meant. "What she doesn't know won't hurt us."

Vivian and Rachel both shrugged and spread their hands as Freyda looked to them, as though to say "Well, what can you do?" Harper felt a small glow of satisfaction at that. She wasn't useless. She wasn't going to sit around waiting for the real heroes to stand up.

"When do we leave?"

3

I remembered hot metal rain and how the glass seemed to shatter in slow motion. I remembered pain. Anguish. Horror.

We'd been driving back to Wylde after fighting and defeating Ethan, a sorcerer doing terrible things to shifters in a bid to gain immortality for his lover. Once we hit regular roads I'd gone to sleep.

Screeching metal woke me. The truck or whatever hit us crunched directly into the side of our truck. My side. Metal screamed and bent inward as our truck flipped off the road and down an embankment.

The saddest words in any language are "what if" and "if only." What if I had been awake? If only I hadn't just spent multiple days burning my magic at both ends so to speak. If only I'd somehow reacted faster.

I remembered reaching for my magic and the razor-sharp pain of it in my veins as I tapped a well not yet replenished. The world went upside-down a final time and we hung in our seatbelts. Alek's face turned to mine, blood from lacerations flowing down into his hair.

That's when the shooting started. Before we could say a word to each other. Before I could free us from our tangled seatbelts. Alek's face so close to mine. His blood dripping. My blood dripping into my eyes. Then hot metal shattering what was left of us. What was left of our world.

I tried to push my body over his but there wasn't room. I got a shield up but it buckled as bullet after bullet found ways through, each a knife of white-hot pain. I was too weak, too hurt. Everything was happening too fast.

In the hellscape of my memories, I saw Alek's mouth moving, forming words. One of my arms was trapped against him but the other was free. I pulled at his seatbelt. He couldn't get out, couldn't shift. My magical shield crumpled completely as blood rushed to my head and what was left of the windows blew apart in a renewed onslaught.

Everything slowed, either from adrenaline or perhaps I'd somehow tapped into Tess's talent and actually slowed time. In memory I couldn't tell; all I could see was the image of us hanging, smashed side by side into a bullet-riddled truck cab, the world turning to sparkling razors and flying metal and blood.

So much blood.

Not enough magic.

Perhaps had things been different, I would have remembered it differently. But in this moment, this horror show in my mind that I knew to be too real, I didn't hesitate. Perhaps if I'd been somewhere safe, not magic-less and chained to a bed, there would have been time to soften my psyche, to curb the blow. To pretend I'd hesitated a moment longer.

To pretend I had never hesitated at all.

My D20 talisman hung against my chin, its weight a reminder. A promise. I took it in my free hand, clutching it with numbed fingers. The chain broke with a hot burn against my neck as I shoved it into my mouth. I felt the hard gem of Samir's heart against my tongue.

The world sped up. Alek's voice suddenly there but buried in the incredible cacophony of what seemed like hundreds of guns firing at once. I reached for a rising swell of power like nothing I'd felt since my time inside the Veil with my birth father.

Then the world exploded as a bullet hit the back of my head and the power slid away into darkness like an ocean wave sucking back out of reach, taking Alek and the world, my world, with it.

"All caught up, then?" Samir said. His face loomed above mine. I was awake again in the white room.

I didn't know how long I'd screamed until the memory had faded, but my throat was a gravel road. He wouldn't let me stay in the peaceful darkness of true unconsciousness, dragging me back again and again to the memory as I looked at every angle, trying to find a way through. To find a way to disprove it.

Alek could not be gone. I didn't care about bullets and logic and what I'd seen. Memories lie, and Samir was inside my mind, doing Universe-knew-what to my head. I didn't know how Alek could have survived, or where he was, but I would find him. I'd raise his ass from the dead if I had to.

"Ah, sticking with denial, are you?"

I turned my face away from Samir, staring into the white nothingness of the wall, watching Alek's blood dripping down his face, seeing the pain in his eyes as he tried to tell me he loved me one last time.

If I'd acted faster. If I'd just eaten Samir's heart from the damn start. Who cared about the state of the world if everyone I loved was gone? Alek wasn't some prize I'd won for being a badass. He was my partner, sometimes my conscience, usually my better half. I'd failed to protect him. And I was trapped here, chained to this bed for who knew how long, while who knew what was happening to the rest of my loved ones.

Agent Ainsley chose that moment to return. Perhaps she thought all the screaming had been for her.

I stared at her with bleary, raw eyes.

"Where is Alek?" I asked.

Something in her gaze flickered, but she quickly pasted back on her stern look. The raw lump that was my heart started crawling toward my throat.

"Hand over Samir's heart and you can see him," she said with a tight smile.

"How about I see him and then I hand over the heart?" I countered.

Agent Ainsley's gaze flickered again and lines formed around her mouth. "You are not in a position to bargain."

"Ask for proof of life," Samir said, his smirk back.

"Show me he's alive and we'll start talking," I ground out through clenched teeth, hating to do what Samir suggested purely because he had suggested it even though it was reasonable.

"Now, Ms. Crow, you need to show signs of cooperating, and then perhaps I can help you."

"Where. Is. Alek?" I said, spitting each word out individually.

"He's very safe," she answered in the least convincing tone imaginable for even though I desperately wanted to believe those words, her pale face and strained voice gave them a lying feel. "You'll see him soon if you just help us. Help us help you."

"Proof of life, then we deal." More like, "proof of life and then I break the fuck out of here and burn down this place and salt the earth," but I managed to restrain myself from saying all that. My throat hurt too much.

"I am going to explain this so you understand," Agent Ainsley said, her eyes going flat and her lip curling slightly. "You have no power here other than your knowledge of where Samir's heart is. We need it as a matter of National Security." She said the words like they were uppercase and underlined. "You start cooperating or things will go very badly for you. We can reach everyone you love, and there are many, very legal, ways to ruin lives. And, of course, less legal ones."

My mind blanked for a white-hot second as rage and frustration finally spilled over. Alek had to be alive. He had to.

"Like shooting the shit out of two civilians and then chaining me to a bed? How long has it been? And don't look at me like that, I was going to remember at some point, you fucking psycho bitch." I strained against my chains. "You think I'm going to bargain with you without proof of life? After what you fuckers did to us? Get bent."

Agent Ainsley backed away from the bed as I snarled the final words out and collapsed back.

"I will see what I can do," she said. She turned and fled the room.

"What the fuck is going on?" I muttered. She'd

looked… terrified? If—no, no *if*—Alek was alive, and he had to be, damnit, why wouldn't she be using him as a bargaining piece right from the start? What were the damn government people playing at? So many things felt… wrong.

"Perhaps he is dead," Samir said.

"Perhaps you should shut the fuck up and die already."

"Your attitude is not improving," Samir said with a mocking shake of his head. "I think we should review that memory."

"Don't you fucking…" But it was too late. Samir's face filled my vision and then darkness claimed me, pulling me down into the nightmare again.

Pulling me back to sheering metal, hot rain, and glass shattering in slow motion as the world turned to blood and pain and broke around me.

And again.

Again.

4

At first I fought him. I tried to wake myself from the nightmares, but when that failed, I reached for my own memories, memories of happier times with friends Samir didn't know and couldn't hurt anymore. Gaming with Harper and the twins. Eating Sunday dinners at Rosie's. Samir always wrestled back control of my dreams, of my memories, dragging me back into the nightmares again and again as punishment every time I managed to stall him.

So I started trying to return to the snowy field below Juniper College. To the day I'd bested his ass once and for all. Well, his physical ass, anyway. He relived his own defeat a dozen times before I grew too weak, too tired to keep us there.

There was no waking. He punished me for those memories with images of Alek broken and bloody, hanging upside down and dying in the truck over and over.

Samir wouldn't let me wake up, and eventually I grew too exhausted by the dreams to fight him. He was a memory ghost, a parasite in my mind. For all I was functionally immortal, I was not indestructible. I was capable of exhaustion, of pain, of weakness and despair, and he exploited every falter, every bruise and scar.

Samir was proving just as dangerous to me dead as he had been when he was alive. Worse, perhaps. For when he'd lived, I'd had allies, friends he could hurt, yes, but people who had helped me fight him. Helped me remember why I fought.

I was so tired that it was hard to remember the faces of people who, I hoped and prayed, lived on. The reasons I had to win, to stop him somehow. They say what doesn't kill you makes you stronger, but it's a lie.

What doesn't kill you can break you, and broken can be so much worse than dead.

He wore me down with the nightmare memories, people I loved dying amid fire and hot metal rain.

Then he finally let me breathe, pulling me into memories of him, times before I'd opened Bluebeard's closet and found the treasure-trove of murder and betrayal.

I wasn't certain which was worse: living and reliving running down the empty halls of the school trying to get to my found family before the bomb, or living and reliving the terrible moments hanging upside down in the truck as bullet after bullet stole the life from Alek. Stole us from each other.

Or that I started to feel grateful when Samir let it stop. That I quit fighting the good memories, those brief times of respite. Cups of tea on a lazy Sunday morning in bed. The first time I levitated a car. Memories full of joy before it turned sour. Because for all I now hated Samir with every last fiber of my being, I never would have stuck with him if it had been all bad. Or even mostly bad. Looking back over the years, the warning signs had all been there, of course. His intense anger when questioned. His lack of speaking about the past. How even the bad things in his past that he did choose to speak about were someone else's fault, but anything good in his life was deserved and clearly his own doing. The way he'd doled out information and knowledge about sorcerers and magic like a controlling parent handing out Halloween candy well into December.

And there was the beach. We returned to the shore of Lake Michigan a lot, though I started to notice that Samir took us away from that memory quickly, never letting it fully play out. Somewhere in the back of my exhausted, grieving mind, I made a note. A note for another time. For another, stronger Jade.

Finally, perhaps because even Samir's ghost had his limits, I woke. The room was exactly the same, a never-changing prison. I tugged weakly at my chains, the mage-bracelets cutting into my sore wrists.

"Stop that," Samir said. My arms dropped of their own accord and I froze. Samir chuckled. "I meant that to be more of a surprise, but we are progressing nicely."

My left big toe wiggled and I tried to make it stop. Samir laughed. He wiggled my toe again and then subsided, leaning on the edge of the bed.

"Where is Ainsley?" I muttered, unable to fully feel the horror of this new development.

So what if Samir could make my body twitch, I wasn't going anywhere. I knew I should feel more… more anything. But it was as though my mind had gone numb in response to the torture, the soft moments and the horrors. The lack of the control. I licked dry, cracked lips. I didn't know how long it took to heal an exploded head, but I was guessing it had been a while, weeks even, since… well, since. I shoved the memory away while I still had that much control. While I still had any choices at all.

Awake, even with Samir watching me and making various fingers and toes wiggle like a child prodding a dead toad with electric wires, I felt clearer than I had while caught in the whirlwind of memory and unconsciousness. I replayed my conversations with Agent Ainsley, because those were safer, more immediate. I returned to my suspicion that Noah Grey was involved. Who else would have told them about the heart? But I had little to go on and less idea how to use that information against her.

"You are doing far too much thinking," Samir said. My toes curled painfully and my right calf cramped.

"Where did the government get these mage-bracelets?" I asked, though I didn't expect an answer. "You made them, but I don't think you'd hand over something that could stop your magic to the U.S. government."

"Ah, assumptions. You truly think I am stupid enough to create something that could stop my magic?"

No, I fully believed that he would have built a fail-safe into them somehow. Or made himself immune. He was dead, his memories were mine, and somewhere in them was the key to these bracelets.

"You just cannot accept that you have lost, can you?" Samir said.

I closed my eyes, willing my mind to find the memories I wanted. All I saw was the red-veined backs of my eyelids.

Ainsley had been frightened, or at least very nervous about me regaining my memories. There was a thread there, if I could grasp it and pull. How was she or whoever she worked for connected to the Archivist? This whole situation didn't feel bureaucratic enough for government work. It was messy. A hit job without a clear plan.

Not Noah either, then. But he would have had the means to acquire the mage-bracelets. He knew about Samir's heart. He'd already tried to manipulate Ethan into getting it for him. He had likely sent the damn agents to my shop as well.

I caught that thread. Why would they come to my shop? Those two, they were government all the way through. Signing dotted lines and making copies in triplicate in their sleep probably. Had someone up the chain gotten impatient?

"This is getting you worked up. Time for a nap I think," Samir said. I felt the darkness rising.

Soon there would be pain again. Or perhaps a lack of it, which was almost worse. I was starting to crave those moments, to wish I wouldn't wake to a world where Alek had become Schrödinger's cat. Alive? Dead? I had no way to open that box.

At least in my dreams, trapped in my memories, I could forget sometimes how helpless I was. How lost. But to surrender was too much like defeat.

"Did you ever meet Noah Grey?" I asked Samir, trying to stall.

"Enough," he said.

But he was right. It was enough. His ghost pulled me into my mind but a flicker of memory there held the vampire's face and I leapt for it, falling down and down as my mind slid away from Samir's grasp and into his memory.

They were in a restaurant; I knew it from the

murmur of voices beyond the heavy velvet curtain shielding their table from view and the almost overwhelming smells of cooked meat, of garlic and onion. I tried to ignore my own sudden, gnawing hunger and focused on the scene. Noah Grey sat in his usual way, perfectly, unnaturally still, a study of a human instead of a living creature with tics and blinks and movement. It was as though he wasn't trying to appear mortal because he knew he didn't need to.

Samir set an ornately carved box on the table. I knew in the way of dreams, or perhaps because I was inside his memories and therefore his mind somehow, that it held the same mage-bracelets that circled my current real-life wrists.

The Archivist did not nod so much as slightly incline his head, but one of the men in a suit stepped forward and opened the box. He rotated it so Noah could see inside, and then, at another dip of the vampire's head, the suit closed the box, picked it up, and stepped back. A second suit came forward and placed an envelope on the table.

"Those will not work on me, in case you had that notion," Samir said. He made no move toward the envelope and instead lifted his tumbler of scotch to his lips with an appreciative inhalation. Rubbing in, at least in his mind, that he could enjoy something like a very fine liquor while the vampire could not. For Samir, being petty wasn't just a brand, it was an art form.

"Goodbye, Samir," Noah Grey said as he rose from the table. He gave Samir a very small smile that was there and gone again in the space of a breath. His eyes almost held pity, but I would have put money on it being contrived or perhaps in my imagination. The vampire enjoyed being the spider in the web, but even he could not have foreseen Samir's end.

Probably. Leaving that thought alone, I walked toward the table but my hand passed right through the envelope.

Noah and his suits left. Samir sat staring at the envelope for a long moment, rolling the tumbler in his hands. Finally he opened it, sliding out a single piece of paper with a photograph attached.

My photograph. A Polaroid taken candidly of me exiting my shop. Looking at the door and my hair and clothing, I knew it was from years ago. Not too long after I'd arrived in Wylde. The paper underneath had my name—my real name that Samir had not, at that point known—and my address.

"Where in hell is Wylde, Idaho?" Samir muttered. "And just what have you been up to, Jade Crow?"

The memory shimmered, the air growing colder as Samir turned in his chair and the restaurant sounds and smells faded back.

"Spying on me?" he said with a sickening smile. "Well, I hope this was illuminating."

"It was," I said, backing away from him even though there was nowhere to go. It had been very illuminating. I'd already suspected the vampire's hand in my current situation, even though it felt too messy for his direct involvement. Noah had always seemed to know more about me than I did and to always be a step ahead, or sometimes playing games we didn't even know we were a part of. Four dimensional chess had nothing on the damn vampire.

"He led you to your death," I added. "Wonder how that feels?"

"Better and better each day," Samir said. The air grew even colder and the restaurant faded completely, turning once again to the beach on Lake Michigan.

I stood there in the cold, rubbing my arms as the wind cut through my sweater and bit into my ungloved hands.

"You could have just left me alone, but I guess that never occurred to you, did it?" I couldn't bring myself to look at him and instead stared at the surfers fighting the slushy brown waves.

"So you could get even stronger and kill me more easily? I am sure you would have preferred that." Samir stepped up beside me, but his body gave off no warmth.

"It's not *Highlander*, damnit," I growled at him. My hands were freezing.

"Oh? And how many mages have you met and allowed to live?"

I opened my mouth. Closed it again.

"That's not fair," I said finally. "They tried to kill me or hurt people I love. I would have lived and let live otherwise."

"Yes, all very justifiable, I am sure. It always is." Samir's coat rustled as he shrugged.

"Why do I keep coming back here?" I asked, changing the subject before he started sounding reasonable.

"Let us go somewhere warmer—bed perhaps? I recall you bought some lovely red lingerie one year for my birthday."

"No," I muttered, only half hearing him. Something about this beach was important. Or something about that memory. Why else would my brain drag me here over and over whenever I gained some control or felt at my most vulnerable?

If only my hands weren't so damned cold.

Cold like they had been that day on the beach. I'd forgotten my gloves.

"I picked up a stone," I said as I bent and imitated the memory from decades past. The stone was smooth and cold in my hand. "I used magic to warm it." I couldn't do that now, but I let the memory in and the stone warmed on its own.

"Jade, stop," Samir said, his voice sharp.

I turned toward him as the stone grew hotter and hotter. We were in the memory now, ghost-Samir losing control as memory-Samir pulled him in. He had been frightened that day. And so angry.

I'd heated the stone too hot and used too much power. I didn't have great control then. The stone was white-hot in my hands and then it started to melt, growing misshapen.

Samir grabbed a ball of icy water from the lake and drenched my glowing hands in a cloud of steam.

I blinked, clearing that steam from my eyes as water beaded on my lashes and ran down my cheeks. In my palms lay the melted stone. In my unburned, completely whole palms.

I had not known what such a thing meant all those years ago. But now, standing there on that beach as ghost-Samir and memory-Samir both stared at me in fear and horror, my memory showed me the key to freedom.

I wasn't just a sorceress.

I was a motherfucking dragon.

Harper

Since they knew the exit roads from the Den were being watched by shifters loyal to the First, Vivian, Harper, and Sheriff Lee, who kept insisting that Harper call her Rachel, had gone on foot for the first part of the journey. Turned out that when the Den had been built, a tunnel had been installed. The exit hadn't been found yet by the enemy, and Freyda was keeping the knowledge very need-to-know in case they had traitors inside the Den. Or in case of mind-control if someone was caught.

Freyda was so paranoid about it that she personally guided the three of them through while they were blindfolded until they were away from the entrance and had made it to a safe house that had been set up between town and the Den. By the time they had wheels and were on the main road, the streets were quiet, a few cars passing as some of the few human denizens of Wylde went about their lives in the evening hours. They'd decided to park at one of the local bars near Vivian's office, hoping to avoid confrontation if any of the First's minions were lurking.

Things had gone smoothly and quietly, Rachel staying outside as a lookout in the shadows of the porch while Harper and Vivian did a fast and dirty job of sacking Vivian's veterinary practice for medical supplies.

"Leave those; we can buy that at Walmart if we need more," Vivian said as Harper went to stuff a container of medical tape and gauze into her duffel bag. "Save room for the good shit."

"Like the morphine and lidocaine?" Harper joked, looking around the supply room. It looked like a tiny tornado had ripped through, a far cry from how it usually was. Harper pushed away the ache of wishing things were different. There was no point dwelling.

"Fridge in my office—here, take the key," Vivian said. She tossed her keyring at Harper.

Square key for the office door, little hexagonal one for the fridge. Harper took a small cooler down from a shelf and started methodically loading it with the precious bottles. She tried not to think about battles to come or medical care that might be needed. With the cooler loaded, Harper flicked the light off, stepped into the hallway, and then froze.

There was a window across from her and the outside of the old Victorian-style house that housed the vet's office was illuminated by the streetlights flickering on in the gathering gloom. Harper stared into that gloom, sure she had seen the shape of a wolf go past.

There it was again, two wolves this time, circling toward the back door. Instinctively Harper pressed her body up against the dark hallway, turning her head slowly toward where Vivian was moving around in the front room.

"Vivian," she hissed, hoping her voice would carry enough to reach the wolf-shifter's keen ears but not give her away to those outside.

Something thunked into the door at the front as though someone had tossed a large rock. Or a body.

"Vivian? Harper? Come out here," Rachel called from somewhere beyond the door. She sounded calm. Too calm. Almost wooden.

Harper forgot to breathe. Her heart stopped beating

as the world went still, the calm before the panic.

"Fuck," Vivian said from the front room.

"They are surrounding the building," Harper said softly as she edged down the hallway toward the vet.

"He's got Rachel," Vivian said, her voice also low, her tone measured, but with the slightest tremor in the words. The words weren't a question. They'd both known the sheriff their whole lives, and though the voice was hers, all of what made Rachel herself was missing.

It wasn't a question of if they could rescue her, but if they could rescue themselves. Vivian didn't look any more ready to debate choices than Harper felt. They'd discussed the risks of coming here. It seemed luck had run out.

"Only two in back, maybe three," Harper said as she set down the cooler carefully and drew the Alpha and Omega. "We can go out that way."

She knew from everything Justice May had warned them about that there was nothing to be done once the First was working his mind-control on someone but wait and hope they were freed because he needed room for more victims. Apparently he could only mind control so many at once and from a fairly short range, so he relied on his trusted followers and threats to keep shifters in line once they were caught. If Rachel was being mind-controlled, the First was almost certainly out there with her.

I have the blade. I could end him. Harper choked back a panicked giggle at that thought. Charging into certain doom hoping to win seemed like a poor plan. But a couple shifters, she could handle those.

Maybe.

"Rachel," Vivian called out. "Stay where you are. We're coming out in a moment." Then, more quietly, for Harper's ears only, she murmured, "Go out the side, I'll make a distraction." The tiny veterinarian gave Harper a stern glance as she pulled a baseball bat from behind the front desk and walked toward the door.

"Vivian, no," Harper said, taking a step toward her. There was zero chance she was going to tuck tail and run from this fight. "You are more valuable than I am. The Den needs a doctor."

"Your mama will never forgive me if I get you taken or killed," Vivian whispered, her voice little more than a tense hiss. "And nobody will forgive us if we hand that magic killing sword over to the First."

"Shit." Harper stared at the blade. She'd brought it

as a back-up plan, feeling safer with it and weirdly a little closer to Jade. She hadn't thought it through all the way.

"Vivian? Harper? It is safe. Come outside—I need your help," Rachel called out again in that un-Sherriff-Lee flat tone.

"For once in your life, Azalea MacNulty, do what I say and go!"

Harper went, tears blurring her eyes. She blinked to clear her vision as she made for the window off the hallway, guessing they wouldn't have as many watching the sides when there was a perfectly good rear door. Harper sheathed the sword and flicked the locks off the window, her hands in position to pull it up. She heard Vivian charge out the front door with a bloodcurdling howl. For a bare second, Harper hesitated, torn between her instincts to run and her desire to save her friends. But the feel of the blade at her hip reminded her of the stakes even as she started to turn back toward the front room.

Crashing sounds from the back office where the rear door was made up her mind.

Harper rolled as she sprang through the window, drawing the blade again as she stood up, the sword leaping to her hand like she'd been exiting buildings in this fashion since birth. She saw the blur of a wolf to her right as it sprang, but she was already moving, running forward and sweeping the blade out to catch the wolf in mid-spring. The impact jarred her arm, but she kept her hand on the sword as it sliced cleanly through the wolf's chest, leaving a ribbon of blood in its wake. The wolf dropped to the ground, dead.

Harper kept running. She didn't let herself hesitate or look back as she charged down the street, tears streaming cold down her cheeks in the warm summer evening air.

She didn't stop running until she was at the safe house, the sword still glowing faintly in her cramped fingers. As Freyda stepped from the shadows, Harper sheathed the blade before collapsing into the Alpha of Alphas' strong embrace.

5

I dove into my own mind, shoving away Samir's raging face, pushing down through layers and flitting hints of memory wrapped in dream and exhaustion. I searched for the fire I knew existed somewhere at the core of everything I was, in every, every drop of blood. I wasn't half-mage, half-dragon, after all, any more than I was half-dragon and half-shifter by parentage. I was both. I was all. I was whole.

I called to the fire within.

And the flames answered.

There was no gradual thinning, weakening, like Samir had hinted would eventually happen. Instead the mage-bracelets melted off my wrists, molten metal lighting the bed on fire, filling the cell with acrid smoke. Power unlike I'd felt since the time within the Veil with my father flowed through me and I nearly levitated off the burning bed. Fire cleansed me, stripping away the metal cuffs, the grime of weeks spent lying in the same place. It burned away the thin blanket into instant ashes, leaving me whole and untouched.

My throat felt hoarse as I tried not to breathe the smoke, but vents in the ceiling opened and the smoke was sucked away as an alarm started pealing somewhere beyond the door.

Samir's mind ghost appeared again as the flames died and I found my feet.

"No, this is not right," he said. "We were doing so well."

A low growl caught both of our attention as Wolf appeared behind ghost-Samir. My legs went a little weak with relief and joy, and I didn't think I'd ever been happier to see anyone in my life. Somehow when Wolf was with me, I knew that things would work out, that whatever we faced, we'd solve it.

Samir tried to grab me, but he was in my head, something he had apparently started to forget. His mind-ghost stumbled through me and materialized again. His golden eyes blazed with anger and fear turned his skin ashy. He looked smaller now, no longer a tyrant in my head, just an apparition. A nightmare fading away with dawn. And I knew then, too, how Sarah must have felt as she stood at the heart of the Labyrinth facing down the Goblin King. "You have no power over me," I couldn't resist saying.

Whatever Samir might have said in response was lost as Wolf unhinged her jaw impossibly wide and ate him.

"Good dog," I said as she pressed her head into my chest. Her fur was soft and warm and everything I needed in that moment.

Well, except clothes. And food. And knowing if Alek was alive or dead or where the hell I was.

But leaning into Wolf's warmth was enough as I struggled to adjust to the power raging through my veins. I'd never felt so much magic at once, and it took a few moments of breathing to get a grip on it. Delayed effect of eating Samir's heart, was my guess. My eyes felt like they were full of sand and my legs were rubber, so I continued leaning on Wolf as I stumbled toward the door. For though I felt like I could destroy the world or fly to the moon or whatever else I wanted with the flood of power inside me, my body had still been healing while starved and chained to a bed. Damned mortal coil.

At least my other memory ghosts were very quiet, even Ethan, the newest resident. I felt them lurking in my head, unlike Samir, who seemed to be utterly missing, his memories locked away. I didn't mind, though at some point I knew I'd probably need some of those back, but given how close he'd taken me to the edge of losing myself, I wasn't in a particular hurry for Wolf to disgorge him even if I knew how to make her do so.

The door opened before I could so much as cast a simple knock spell. Agent Ainsley—though I had serious doubts that was her name or title now—burst in with two large men on her heels. I threw myself to the side and flattened against the wall as they pulled up short, all three staring at the empty bed like I'd gone invisible.

"Hi," I said. It was comical how easy it was to unleash power from my hands as I raised them and pushed.

The two men, who both looked like they could audition for bouncer extras in an action movie, flew sideways, knocking into each other and then collapsing against the far wall. I wrapped bands of power around them and tied them off like ropes as they struggled helplessly against my magic. I pulled the bands tight, and they stopped struggling with alarming groans cut off into strained silence. I didn't know if I'd killed them. I didn't know if I cared. It was hard to feel sympathy for people who'd shot me, locked me in a room, and likely had a direct hand in Alek's…

"So, Ainsley, how do you want to do this?" I said to the cringing woman. It was easier to talk than to dwell on thoughts I didn't want to face yet.

"Be reasonable, Jade. Let's talk," Ainsley said. She glanced nervously at the door and jerked upright in surprise as Wolf materialized and growled.

"Sure," I said. "Reasonable, like shooting the shit out of me and my mate? Or perhaps the reasonable you mean is chaining me to a bed and starving me? Which part of that was reasonable, in your mind?" My voice sounded foreign to my ears, cold and scratchy. I wrapped a band of power around Ainsley and lifted her into the air, then slammed her into the wall with a flick of my wrist.

"Stop! Please, you have to understand, I'm just following orders."

"Ah, the 'following orders' defense. How's that worked out for people, historically?" I said as I advanced and brought Ainsley down to her tip-toes so we could stare each other in the eye. My rubbery legs were strengthened with rage.

"You don't need to do this. You don't hurt people like this right? I'm helpless!" Ainsley licked her thin lips as a tear crawled down her cheek.

"I guess it's true—you either die a hero or live long enough to see yourself become the villain," I said, as much for my sake as hers. From the frightened and confused look on Ainsley's face, I guessed she wasn't much of a Batman fan. "You say orders? Who gave you the order?"

"I told you, I work for the government. There will be a lot more of them along in a minute. Please, Jade. I can help you get out of here." She looked wildly around the room and I didn't believe her for a second.

The last sorcerer whose heart I'd eaten—well, before Samir's—had been skilled with mind magic and illusion. I drew on his memories, looking for a way to make Ainsley tell me the truth in the shortest amount of time possible. I didn't know if she was right about more goons coming, but I could feel that the rage and grief and flood of power sustaining me wasn't going to last forever.

Ethan's mind-ghost warned me that if I cracked into Ainsley's mind, she likely wouldn't survive, at least not wholly sane.

I didn't give a flying fuck. This woman was part of whatever had shot me, had hurt and maybe killed Alek. If Alek was dead, if... I was going to go on a revenge spree worthy of John Wick.

It was a little like forming thoughts into a spear tipped with power and driving it through Ainsley's forehead. From the sounds she started making it must have hurt. Spit flecked her lips and sprayed onto my face, but I kept pushing.

"Tell me the truth. Show me," I demanded.

There was a sickening popping noise that I was only mostly sure was in our heads, and I was inside her mind, slamming into her memories like a wrecking ball.

Her mind wasn't my mind, so a lot of things I saw made no sense. Ethan's mind-ghost was there in my head, whispering advice on what to look at and what to let go, how to keep myself whole inside the maelstrom of images and shadows and words. It would have been easy to get lost, but my power held me together in its blade, and my question to Ainsley brought to the forefront her answer, hanging like the proverbial fruit for plucking.

At the center of that rotten fruit was the damn vampire. And a tale of overreaching minions and incompetence that was almost insulting in its effectiveness at putting me in the current situation. Sometimes life hands you masterminds and dastardly plans. Sometimes it just hands you assholes who get lucky.

She'd been in charge of the team monitoring Ethan. When he'd failed, she was supposed to report back to Noah Grey. However, being the ambitious minion she was, Ainsley figured she could salvage things and capture me. So she called in the cavalry, which in this case was a couple truckloads of men with a lot of guns, and ambushed us. The whimpering woman flattened to the wall in front of me was directly responsible for Alek's death. For Samir's near-takeover of my body and mind. For every shitty moment of mental and physical torture I'd undergone for who knew how long.

I almost pulled back and smashed her into freezer

jam right then, but an image of Alek being worked on by what looked like medical staff held me back.

"He's not dead," Ainsley moaned. "He's alive."

The Archivist, Noah Grey, himself had shown up and he'd been livid. Well, as livid as his un-emotive ass got. I could see the anger in his flat eyes, the look of a predator about to end an annoyance. But Ainsley had begged for another chance, had pointed out that they could trick me when I healed and perhaps get me to reveal the information in exchange for Alek's life.

If he lived. Which he had. The Archivist had him and had given Ainsley a reprieve if she could get me to tell them where Samir's heart was. This was her final chance to save her skin and redeem herself in the vampire's eyes, though I had a feeling that she was going to be history either way. Noah Grey didn't seem the type to suffer ambitious fools for very long.

Alek was alive. Ainsley hadn't told me that yet because I didn't have my memories, so she'd tried a different tactic, thinking she could trick me into revealing where Samir's heart was by acting like the government. Like I would have ever handed something that dangerous over to anyone, much less the United States government. Ainsley clearly hadn't studied history, especially indigenous history, if she thought that was ever gonna happen.

Alek was alive. The knowledge took a moment to truly sink in. Alek was alive. There was nothing sweeter in the world than those words.

"Alek is alive," I shouted aloud as I left Ainsley's mind and memories. I staggered back as the real world reasserted itself like someone had turned off the speakers at a chaotic concert: all the noise and imagery and pressure went with a whoosh.

I promised myself that I was done with being stuck in my head or anyone else's memories after this. Maybe. Hopefully. I'd had quite enough of living in memory and dream. I was going to rescue Alek, find my friends, and then hold them close forever.

She sagged to the floor and touched her bleeding nose. I had been both right and wrong about the vampire's involvement. It was too messy for him, because he hadn't come up with this shit plan, but he was still all over it in his own way. At its core, this was all his fault. He was the one keeping Alek prisoner and at the moment that was all that mattered to me.

I didn't have to ask where we were. I knew from her mind that we were in an abandoned meat-packing facility to the south of Seattle they had quickly refurbished to be my recovery room-slash-prison. Alek was miles and miles away, but not for long.

"You're going to take me to Noah Grey," I said. Ainsley had a car here, and I didn't feel like driving myself. Trying to stay upright was about all I could manage physically at the moment.

"Okay," Ainsley said after she worked her jaw around as though she had more to say but thought better of it. I knew from her mind, too, that there were no more goons coming. She was all alone with me now. Lucky her.

"You ever seen the movie *Scanners*?" I asked as she got to her feet.

She nodded, the confused look back at war with the fear in her eyes.

"Good. 'Cause if you do anything stupid, that's what will happen," I said. I made an explosion gesture with my hands to each side of my head.

Ainsley swallowed hard and looked as though she might vomit.

"Also, I need clothes," I said, looking her up and down pointedly.

She looked down at her white lab coat and pinstriped

slacks. "I have spare clothes in my car," she said as she wrapped her arms around over her chest.

"Lead the way," I said, deciding that would do. Clean clothes sounded like heaven. Wolf disappeared from the doorway, and I followed Ainsley out.

The fresh power in my blood still simmered, the dragon just below the surface, a burning strength waiting to be unleashed. Ainsley, Noah Grey, Samir... they had all underestimated what I would and could do to protect the people I loved. I had failed so many times. Not today.

Today I was bringing the reckoning. "Hold tight, Alek," I murmured. "I'm your ride home, and I'm almost there."

6

I was somehow unsurprised that Ainsley had a full change of clothes, right down to shoes, in her car. I wasn't surprised she drove a BMW either. Her shoes didn't fit me, but her spare suit hung on my newly gaunt frame. I was grateful that belts were back in style. I made do with socks, since shoes two sizes too small were never going to happen and I wasn't sure how quick on my feet I would need to be. Hopefully not very. Magic still raged in my blood, but my body sank into the overpriced leather seats like a cat falling into a beanbag.

Ainsley also didn't have a cell phone on her. Which did surprise me. I wouldn't have believed her, but I still held the remnants of her memories in my head like visual tracers from staring too hard into a bright light, so I knew she wasn't lying. She had forbidden all such things from the facility out of fear someone might trace them. It was gratifying that she thought I had connections powerful enough to do that and humbling that I didn't at the same time.

The advantage was that she had no way to tell the Archivist I was coming. The disadvantage was that I had no way to contact Harper or Ezee and Levi or Lara and get help. I was on my own. Ainsley knew nothing about what might be happening back in Wylde, but I'd been down and out for over two weeks and I wasn't sure if the First would sit on his proverbial hands that long. Though if it was Alek he wanted, us being gone from Wylde might have helped. That was another Schrödinger's box to be opened later.

First, Alek. Then I could worry about home. We left the abandoned facility and drove into the night, merging into the traffic heading north to Seattle. I didn't dare let my guard down, though the woman beside me seemed to have taken my head-exploding threat very seriously. She hardly made a sound as we drove, her hands at ten and two, her eyes glued to the road. Every now and again her tongue flicked nervously over her lips, but that was about the only sign of life other than her heavy breathing.

Turned out we didn't have to tell the Archivist we were coming. In true Noah fashion, he was ready and waiting. Perhaps he'd been waiting, or more likely he had cameras on the approach road and a tracker in Ainsley's car. If I'd been less exhausted and angry, I would have checked for that. Hindsight etc.

The warehouse stood next to the sound, a dark two-story building with its now-familiar heavy steel door. Ainsley started to turn into the parking lot, but I stopped her.

"This is far enough," I said, staring out the windshield at our welcome crew.

Noah Grey stood in the parking lot on one side of a bright white line of paint. He was alone as far as I could see, no signs of movement anywhere other than a light breeze stirring the trees that lined the roadside edge of the lot.

"Get out and walk ahead of me," I told Ainsley. I gathered my magic, ready for anything, and climbed out of the car. Ainsley followed more slowly. I had a feeling she wasn't looking forward to facing her boss with the evidence of yet another failure in tow.

Ainsley gave me one last nervous look and bolted toward the warehouse. So much for walking ahead of me. Nobody shot at her and no landmines went off, not that I'd really expected something so obvious. That was more Ainsley's style, not the vampire's.

"I'm here for Alek," I said as I walked slowly toward the Archivist. I was stating the obvious, but I figured I'd make sure we were on the same page. "I've had a bad couple weeks and I won't be taking questions or bullshit at this time," I added as Ainsley tried to say something.

Noah moved in a blur. I threw a shield up, but there was no point. With a quick, efficient twist, the vampire snapped Ainsley's neck and threw her body a dozen feet behind him, where it fetched up against the side of the building in a white, crumpled heap.

I went for the door while he was mildly distracted. And slammed into an invisible wall.

As I picked my dignity and my ass up from the pavement where the recoil had thrown me, Noah chuckled.

"A little blood is a powerful thing," he said. He was back to standing on the other side of the brightly painted line, smoothing his shirt cuffs down as though killing Ainsley had been a minor inconvenience to his wardrobe.

I slammed my palms against the invisible barrier. It was like hitting a slightly warm stone surface. I pushed pure power into it and nearly ended up on my ass again as the barrier reflected my magic back at me. The white line extended around the building as far as I could see, and I didn't want to walk the whole perimeter without shoes on except as a last resort. Noah Grey didn't leave loose ends that obvious anyway.

But maybe I could go under it. Or perhaps over. I looked up, then realized my line of thinking was obvious and refocused on the vampire.

A hint of a smile touched his cold mouth. "Not under or over, either. There is only one way you and Aleksei will be reunited, Jade."

"You want Samir's heart," I said, folding my arms over my chest.

Noah inclined his head. "I do. Change is coming. I always feel it when eras begin and end. I have decided Samir's heart is too precious to be left in your volatile hands."

"So much safer with you, who definitely won't sell

it to the highest bidder," I said. My skin itched with magic and the desire to keep blasting away at this stupid ward until the vampire was a smoking ruin and Alek and I were making out like teenagers in the rubble.

"I like the way the world is. And in the end, this is immaterial. Aleksei for the heart." Noah watched me with flat silver eyes as I stepped up until my nose nearly hit the barrier.

"How do I know Alek is okay and that you'll uphold your part of the deal? Your minions shot us up, remember? Oh, and there was that little thing with the insane Ethan guy. You aren't exactly on my 'most trusted' list at the moment."

"What you believe or not does not concern me. I imagine you know Alek is alive because Ainsley told you."

Which he'd expected, I realized. As always, the vampire hedged his bets. If Ainsley succeeded, he'd have the heart and then could dispose of me in some gruesome way, much like I'd held Samir in limbo probably. If—or, rather, I think he knew when—Ainsley failed, well, he had Alek and a ward designed specifically to keep me out, made with the drops of blood I'd traded him years ago.

"Or you let Alek go and we call it even. I go live my life and you live your un-life and we agree to never meet again." I bared my teeth at him in my best fake smile.

"Alek for the heart, Jade. That is the deal."

I slammed another wave of magic in the barrier in frustration and ended up skidding halfway across the parking lot. Ainsley's spare socks didn't hold up so well to being dragged across pavement, and my feet stung where holes had formed in the thin material. My legs locked up in sympathy as I staggered back toward the vampire. My body was hitting all its limits, no matter how much magic raged inside my veins. I was still half-starved and running on the fumes of frustration and anger. And maybe a little fear. Which I wasn't about to admit to. I blinked back tears and punched the barrier lightly. Even that stung.

"It is a hard lesson to accept," Noah said. "But there is always something out there more powerful than you, Jade. Take my deal, get your lover back, and know that you will live to fight another day. You cannot win every battle."

"Do you keep a notebook of affirmations and shitty

sayings next to your coffin?" I muttered. "Or is your brain so calcified by undeath that you think you sound wise right now?"

"The heart, Jade." Noah's mouth pressed into a thin line and his silver eyes narrowed.

I knew I shouldn't poke the vampire, not while he held Alek's life in his hands. If I'd had Samir's heart, I might have handed it over, not gonna lie. There was just a pesky, tiny problem. Samir's heart was my heart now, and I wasn't about to hand that over.

Not yet, anyway. Only as a last resort.

"I don't exactly have it on me," I said. Not technically a lie.

"Alek has enjoyed my hospitality long enough, I think. You will come back at midnight tomorrow. I would not recommend being late."

"Wait," I called out as the vampire turned and walked toward the door. Two men in suits came out and went for Ainsley's body. "That's not enough time. I don't even have money on me to get home." I had no idea what was waiting for me in Wylde, or how to fool the damn vampire into taking a fake heart, or how to bring down the barrier.

"You are resourceful, Jade Crow. Get it done,"

Noah said over his shoulder before he disappeared into the building.

Fuck my life, I thought. Alek was so close and yet he might as well have been on the moon for all I could reach him.

This was a setback, but I had to find a way out. A fake heart, perhaps. Something. I walked back to the BMW. Ainsley had left the keys in the ignition, Universe bless her. It would be a long drive back to Wylde and I wasn't sure I was up for it. I hunted around in the car for a wallet or loose change, but Ainsley must have had her wallet on her and her body had disappeared into the warehouse beyond the ward.

I started driving anyway, heading into Seattle toward lights and noise and humans. It was time to find out what was happening in Wylde. I finally found a parking spot and let my head rest against the steering wheel for a long moment. Noah had called me resourceful, so I took stock of my resources.

I had less than half a tank of gas, an exhausted body, a probably Lo-Jacked car, and no idea how I was going to fake Samir's heart and get my mate out alive. I had the memories of half a dozen sorcerers and assorted magic-users in my head, including a necromancer. I didn't have access to Samir's memories at the moment.

Necromancer. Right. Except my magic couldn't penetrate the barrier ward thingy and I doubted I could get Noah to come out. He wouldn't be tricked easily. So former necromancer now mind-ghost Robert Loughlin's knowledge wasn't likely to help unless he knew some indirect way to control a vampire. I searched as quickly as I could through his memories, my mind recoiling from the decaying, sickly-sweet feel of them. Everything Robert knew about vampires was from moldering books and what little he'd managed to get out of the vampire Ishimaru when he had the latter enslaved. His obsession had been raising a vampire named Lilith from some kind of eternal sleep her own children had put her into, according to some sketchy tomes the necromancer had bought off an old woman in a cave in Greece.

Lilith, the original vampire. Supposedly the Mother of All Vampires from what Robert had researched. Imprisoned and forced into slumber by nine of her children.

In Idaho. At an intersection of powerful ley lines less than an hour outside of Wylde. And Robert had done most of the research needed to figure out how—

potentially anyway—to raise her back to the living. Well, to the undead. He had stalled out because he'd been unable to find blood powerful enough and he'd been worried he couldn't manage the complexity of the spells needed to control her so he could strike his bargain for eternal life.

"Always someone more powerful than you," I said aloud. The plan forming in my mind was a terrible plan but it was my plan, damnit, and I wasn't exactly overflowing with better ideas.

And there was one other resource I had, or at least I hoped I still had. Friends.

I climbed out of the BMW and went looking for someone, anyone, who would loan me their phone.

Harper

Harper wasn't sure which was worse: that no one blamed her or berated her for what had happened with Vivian and Rachel, or that there had been little time to dwell on the consequences since she'd returned. A part of her wanted to wallow in her failure and misery, but upon her return to the Den with Freyda, they'd been greeted with the good news that Brie and Ciaran had not only returned, but had made it safely to them.

The good news turned out to be mixed. Harper joined Freyda, Rose, Junebug, Ezee, Levi, and Iollan out in front of the Den, where Brie and Ciaran explained that the First had cut his own deal with the Fey.

"So we cannot interfere with him. We're to stay out of shifter affairs," Ciaran said with a pained look that conveyed all of his disgust for the deal.

"Out of direct interference," Brie added. She looked more amused than annoyed.

"What are you proposing?" Freyda asked.

Turned out that Brie, with Iollan and Ciaran's help, could set up a ward around the Den that would allow only those she permitted to pass through. As she put it, "It isn't interfering. I have a right to protect where I live and I like this place just fine. Think I'll make it our summer home—what do you say, Ciaran?"

The druid, the leprechaun, and the baker walked down the hill with linked hands. The tiny hairs on the back of Harper's neck rose and the sweet smell of baking bread wafted on the breeze. Their three red heads turned to glowing like fire in the setting sun as pale lights flickered to life around them. The huge druid went to his knees, and Ezee made a nervous sound beside Harper, but it seemed Iollan had only done so to bring his height closer to the other two. A soft hum vibrated across the distance and the three raised their linked arms to the sky.

Though the triumvirate at the bottom of the hill stood linked like this for what felt like hours and the others returned to their duties, Harper and the twins kept vigil in near silence. Her mom paused before leaving, and squeezed Harper's arm gently then made a slight motion with her head toward the door, but Harper shook her head. Inside it was too easy to dwell on things Harper didn't want to stare down just yet. With another squeeze, Rose let go and went inside, leaving Harper and the twins alone.

She let herself lean against the wall of the Den as she watched, keenly aware that Ezee and Levi had moved to flank her on either side. They stood close, not quite touching, but she felt the warmth of their bodies. Nearby and comforting without smothering. From time to time she glanced at them, afraid of what she'd see in their dark eyes, but each time their gazes were fixed on the field and the magic being worked below.

The evening sunlight was long gone, no trace of pink or orange on the horizon, and the figures below were limned only with a glitter of magic. Stars winked into being and the wind died down to a whisper. Then the glitter of magic shifted away from the three below and lifted like a net into the sky. For the space of a breath, the whole sky above the Den was full of gleaming fairy lights, and then it was gone in a blink, leaving starlight and darkness in its wake.

"It is done," Iollan said as the three of them returned from below. He leaned down and kissed Ezee's forehead.

"No one can come in without permission now?" Harper asked.

"No one," Brie said with a tired nod.

"But what if Jade needs to get in? Or Alek?" Harper forced the words out, making herself ask the question she knew they all wanted to the answer to.

Brie shook her head. "I do not know what has happened to Jade, but something has changed. The Fey Council is frightened. The world feels different today than it did even weeks ago, though I cannot pinpoint why as yet."

"We do not know what has happened, but Jade is strong," Ciaran added quickly. "When the time comes, we will be here to bring them through the ward. Do not trouble yourself, Azalea. Come inside."

Iollan, Ciaran, and Brie went in but Harper hung back, staring out into the darkness. Ezee and Levi both turned back and held out their hands.

"What if she's really gone?" Harper said the words quietly as though saying them too loudly might make it true all on its own. She fingered the hilt of the Alpha and Omega. All they knew of Jade and Alek's fate was bullet-ridden metal and fragments of bone. And so much blood. Too much.

"We don't know she's gone, so no point dwelling on it," Levi said. "Jade's basically immortal, remember?"

"But not totally immortal. And Alek is just like us." Harper lost the battle against her tears. They blurred her vision and traced hot lines down her cheeks. "You heard Brie. Maybe we have to accept that Goku isn't coming back to save us this time."

It was easier to get those words out than to say that Jade was dead. It was too much to say aloud that her friend was gone. Too hard to accept that there would be no sorceress riding to their rescue with some new cool power and a snappy comeback. That Jade would never call her "furball" again. Harper dug her fingernails into her palms but the pain couldn't make her aching heart stop hurting or move the lump forming in her throat.

Ezee and Levi closed ranks around her, sandwiching her between their strong, solid bodies, wrapping her in their arms, their scent, their love and grief. They swayed together as Harper sobbed, clinging to them like a life raft.

"Why do I hear the opening music from *The X-Files*?" Levi said. "Am I losing it?"

Ezee pulled away from them. "It's my ringtone for unknown numbers," he said. "I'll let it go to voicemail."

"We're in a crisis, Ezee. Now is not the time to be screening your calls," Levi said.

Ezee brushed one hand over his own tear-streaked face as he fumbled his phone from his pocket with the other. "Fine. Hello?"

"Ezee? Thank the Universe," came the tinny reply.

Harper froze, refusing to believe her ears. Levi, his arms still around her, lifted her clean off the ground and spun in a half-circle.

"See?" he cried gleefully. "You *never* give up on Goku!"

7

I got lucky that the couple running the convenience store I walked into were Sikhs, and thus not only didn't call the police on the sickly looking brown-skinned woman in an ill-fitting suit and no shoes on, but they let me use their phone and insisted I drink a Coke before I left. It was nice to be reminded after my ordeal that there were good people in the world, too.

Iollan had me meet him in a nearby park where apparently the trees were large enough that he could use them to do his druid teleport magic. He came alone, as I'd requested. I figured a full reunion could wait until we weren't in the middle of a city. I hadn't realized how much fear and emotion I'd been holding in until I saw the druid's bearded, craggy face and his gentle arms engulfed me in a hug. I let myself sag against him as relief sapped my remaining strength.

"They'll kill me if I don't get you back quickly," he said. "But are you all right?"

"There's a lot to tell, but it should wait till we're back." I hadn't given much of an explanation over the phone, since I had two very concerned humans hovering over me at the time. Ezee had picked up on the fact that I wasn't alone and we'd managed to convey what I needed without sounding completely bonkers.

Tree-travel had not improved since I'd last done it. The Coke I'd drunk earlier had tasted at the time like the proverbial nectar of the Gods, but after I slammed through space and time inside a network of tree roots via druidic magic, my stomach felt like it was full of battery acid and regret. We emerged inside a familiar stand of trees at the base of the hill where the Den stood and I was immediately mobbed by warm bodies. The air was dark and warm and close, but I didn't mind. A hint of sweetness clung to the breeze along with a feeling of immense power, like the pressure I'd feel when diving into the deep end of the pool. Magic had happened here, maybe still clung, but I was too smothered by friends to get a word out.

"Give her some room to breathe," Ezee said after a full minute of us all smashed together into a giant friend hug. He was the first to pull back, tear of joy and relief in his dark eyes mirroring my own.

Harper kept her arm around me, looking at me like she wasn't sure yet that I was real, but Levi, Lara, and Junebug all stepped back.

"I'm okay, furball," I said, giving Harper a hug all her own. I felt stronger just for being here, though my feet hurt and my head still spun from the tree-travel.

"Where's Alek?" Levi peered behind us as though Alek might be lurking in the dark wood.

"Levi, give her a minute, geez," Lara said.

"It's a long story," I said. "And I don't have much time. Is there somewhere we can talk?" And where I could sit down, though I didn't say that part aloud. I still had some pride, and they were worried enough about me. I also didn't ask why we were at the Den. Ezee had mentioned on the phone that everyone was there, but he'd been reluctant to explain more, and there hadn't really been time anyway.

Iollan carried me up the hill after my feeble protests

were silenced by a glare from everyone else. Freyda, Brie, and Ciaran met us at the top.

"Good to see you back, Jade," Freyda said, offering her hands in greeting as the druid set me on my feet.

"I'm guessing some shit has gone down?" I asked, looking around at the bustle and horde of bodies inside as Freyda led us in. Many unfamiliar faces and a few that I recognized from around Wylde glanced my way as we made our way through the great hall to a small room down a short hallway beyond it. It might have been an office at one point but now it was lined with a few cots and pillows. The room was quite soundproofed: the noise of the people down the short hallway and in the larger rooms beyond dying away as Freyda closed the door.

The room was cramped with all of us inside, but we made do. Ezee and Iollan sat on the floor by the door. Junebug, Levi, and Ciaran took one cot, treating it like a couch. Brie and Freyda shared another cot. Harper, Lara, and I took the remaining cot, them sandwiching me between them. I leaned gratefully against a pillow Harper tucked between me and the wall behind me. My stomach chose that moment to growl.

"Oh, we should let you eat and rest," Lara said, starting to get to her feet again.

"No, there's no time. We have a lot of catching up to do." I pulled her back down.

"I can get what I miss from Brie," Ciaran said, getting to his feet. He stepped over Ezee's legs and was out the door before I could protest.

"I felt magic out there?" I said, looking at the druid.

"We set a ward around the Den," Brie answered. "The First cut a deal with the Fey, and we cannot directly help, but we can keep the First and his minions out of this place at least."

"So the First is here?" I'd guessed something like that must have happened, if everyone was hiding out at the Den. I'd been gone only a few short weeks, but it felt like a lifetime in some ways. I'd felt like I was fighting Samir through many lifetimes of memories which I was sure didn't help. "Where's May?"

"We don't know," Ezee said at the same time that Freyda said, "She left to try to help some shifters fleeing the First."

"We haven't heard from her since." Ezee's face was grim.

"Rachel? Vivian? Rose?" I listed the names of people who weren't in the room who I figured would be in the thick of it here.

"Mom is helping with sorting through supplies," Harper said, her voice rough. "Rachel and Vivian…" She trailed off and tears sprung into her eyes. "I failed them."

"You didn't fail them," Lara said. Ezee and Levi and Junebug all echoed her with protests.

"Tell me everything," I said. "But do it fast."

"Why?" Ezee leveled his keen gaze on me.

"It's a long story, but I've got until midnight tomorrow to return to Seattle and free Alek from the Archivist."

That was met with total silence. A few mouths opened and closed. Brie shook her head with a sigh.

It took another minute of coaxing, but I got the full story from my friends. The First had rolled into town just after Alek and I were gunned down and started taking shifters away with force or mind-control, depending. Justice May had gone out days before to find a group and guide them in, but nobody had heard from her since. Vivian and Rachel had gone on a scouting and medical supply mission with Harper and were now under the control of the First. Harper shivered beside me as they told me that part, and I wrapped an arm around her. The others were right: it wasn't her fault. They'd all known the danger, and ultimately the responsibility rested on the asshole who had mind-controlled them and was fucking up my home.

"Your turn," Levi said with an attempt at his trademark grin.

"We found the truck, saw the carnage there," Ezee said.

"And your necklace," Harper said, sitting up from where she'd been resting on my shoulder. "I thought Samir had somehow escaped and gotten you."

"Yeah, about that," I said, my eyes traveling around the room and finally resting on Brie. She gave me a little nod, as though I had just confirmed something she already suspected. "Samir is dead."

"*Dead* dead?" Levi asked. I was guessing that Harper had filled the twins in on how Samir wasn't totally gone and had been living in my necklace. I should have done it, but given the circumstances I didn't begrudge that she'd taken initiative.

"Wait, I thought he was already dead?" Lara said. Freyda was staring at me with a speculative look. Levi must have told Junebug because she looked unsurprised.

"He was mostly dead, but actually eating his heart would apparently have some serious consequences for the world," I said, still looking at Brie.

Ciaran came back at that moment and caused some shuffling around to happen as the plate of cheese, bread, and sliced apples he'd brought me was handed over.

"But you said he's dead now?" Harper asked, looking intently at me as I stuffed cheese into my mouth and nodded.

I took a solid minute to chew and eat a few bites, thinking about how to tell them I'd sort of maybe ended the world in a way. There was no good way to sugarcoat it, and Brie certainly didn't seem willing to step up and add anything. Her face warred between resignation and eagerness, which given she was three goddesses crammed into one body, was a little worrying on both accounts.

"We were being shot full of holes. I thought we were dying and I was out of juice from the fight with Ethan—the mage in the Frank," I added at the confused looks. "So I ate Samir's heart. About a quarter second before a bullet exploded my head, as far as I can recall."

"And Alek?"

I turned my head to look at Harper as I swallowed another quick bite of apple. "The people who shot us were working for the Archivist, though they went off script and decided to get ambitious. But the vampire saved Alek and is keeping him imprisoned in Seattle. He wants to trade him for Samir's heart." Alek's location was a guess based on the lengths Noah had gone to keep me out of his magic warehouse, but I had to work with what I had.

"But you ate Samir's heart," Levi said.

"Yep. But the vampire doesn't know that. His minions had me locked up in an old meat-packing plant while I healed and have no idea about the whole heart-eating thing." I decided to skip the "Samir's ghost nearly tortured me into losing control of my own body and mind" part for now. We had enough shit on our plates and not enough time to deal with all the problems.

My actual plate was empty somehow. I hadn't had a real meal in forever, and the food sat like a lump in my stomach. There was so much to do, and I wasn't sure I could do it all alone, but the situation here was worse than I'd imagined. I needed to clone myself, then maybe one of me could sleep while the others went off to save everyone.

But the First couldn't get into the Den, thanks to Brie and the triumvirate. Alek had a day until the vampire decided to do something terrible. I wasn't cloned. I could only tackle one life-threatening crisis at a time.

"So you are going to bring him a fake heart?" Lara asked.

"Not exactly," I said. I could feel Brie's gaze on me still and had no idea what she was going to think about waking up another powerful being. Then again, it wasn't my fault that everyone had apparently decided the River of No Return was the place to dump all the ancient evils and what have you. I glanced around at everyone again, avoiding Brie's eyes.

"I should get back to work," Freyda said, interpreting my hesitation as reluctance to speak in front of her.

"That's not necessary," I said.

"Glad to have you back, Jade, but there are things I must do, too. If there's anything you need for getting Alek back, let me know." She left, and silence dropped over the room again. I hoped that Freyda understood

I had to deal with Alek and the vampire before I could even begin to figure out how to save everyone here.

"Will this help?" Harper said. She stood up and started undoing her belt, where a dagger, a very familiar dagger, was strapped.

"Wait, how did you get that? I left it buried under a ton of rock and dirt."

"It just showed up," Harper said.

"No take backs," I said, holding up my hands palm-out. "If the Alpha and Omega chose you, maybe you should hang on to it. Though I reserve the right to borrow it in case I can just stick it up the First's ass and solve this quickly."

"We call him Bob now," Levi informed me. "Big Ol' Bad."

"No we don't," Ezee muttered.

"Right, how are we getting Alek back?" Lara said. I got the impression she'd been playing peacekeeper between the others a lot from the exasperated look on her face.

The only way out was through, as they say.

"I'm going to wake up the Archivist's mom and then ask him again real nicely." Yeah, that plan sounded just as terrible aloud as it had in my head.

"His mom," Ezee deadpanned.

"Seriously?" Harper said.

"Who is his mom? Do vampires even have mothers? Is she a vampire too?" Levi slid his hand into Junebug's, and they exchanged a questioning look.

"Lilith," Brie said softly. "You are talking about waking the Mother of All Vampires."

"Yes," I said, running tired fingers through my hair and finding new tangles as my makeshift braid unraveled. "I'm going to raise her, cut a deal with her, and then I'm gonna ask Noah again very politely for my mate back. Any questions?"

There were a lot of questions, but in the end, as I'd known in my heart would happen, the plan came together and I wasn't going alone to wake a vampire. They say friends help you move, and real friends help you move bodies. But trust me, only the very best of friends help you *raise* bodies.

8

I apparently looked as dead on my feet as I felt, so Harper escorted me under some protest to the room she was sharing with her mom. My friends had a point, however. I wasn't going to be able to keep working magic without some rest and more food in me, and raising a vampire in daylight was probably a bad idea. I wasn't sure how I could rest, not with Alek still imprisoned. At least my dreams would be free of Samir. Small mercies.

Before falling asleep, I made myself walk through every shred of knowledge and memory the necromancer had about Lilith. There wasn't much, except some arcane circle plans and a lot of talk about "blood of power," which I hoped meant mine would do. Even so, I wanted to minimize the amount of time I had to spend keeping Lilith under control if this worked.

There was no point thinking about if it didn't work. I'd figure something out. After all, I was so damned *resourceful*, right?

Curled in the narrow bed that smelled of Harper and summer evenings, I pushed away worries over Alek, over what kind of place he was kept. Caged? Chained?

"One more night, love," I whispered. I knew there was no way he could know this but I hoped in my heart that he would know that I would always come for him. The despair I'd had when I didn't know if he was alive or dead rose like a specter in my memory, despair I hoped he wasn't suffering. Sleep seemed far away, and yet, even as I closed my eyes on unshed tears, exhaustion claimed me.

I slept longer than I meant to, a deep, dreamless sleep with no memory or sorrow haunting the darkness behind my eyelids. The sun was high in the sky behind the blinds and my body felt as though I'd spent a week being run over by a truck, but my mind had fewer cobwebs, and when I tested summoning a little ball of glowing purple light, it didn't hurt a bit. The magic came almost too easily and I had to rein it in. I'd definitely gotten a power-spike, but like over-leveling a character in World of Warcraft, I wasn't quite up on my new powers yet in practice. I closed my hand on the ball and got out of bed.

"Hey," Harper said as she peeked in the door, then came in as she realized I was awake. "These should fit you." She held out a stack of clothes.

"Thanks," I said. I'd taken the world's most luxurious shower before collapsing into bed the night before and only pulled on a loaner oversize teeshirt. I supposed I couldn't go save the world without pants.

"I thought you might want this back," Harper added as I pulled on a pair of jeans. I looked up to see her holding out my D20, newly strung on a piece of leather cord.

Words failed me as I clutched at it and then grabbed her into a hug, fighting tears. That stupid necklace had been with me all the way from New York and my second family. It was all I had of them that wasn't purely memory. Harper pulled away and put the cord over my head. The silver D20 settled into its place against my breastbone, and it was like a piece of me that the guns and Samir had taken was restored. I wasn't whole or healed yet, but I was one step closer to feeling like myself.

"Don't cry, 'cause then I'll cry, and we got shit to do. Like breakfast." Harper squeezed my arms and let me go.

I joined the druid and Ezee at a table and plowed my way through a plate of toast and eggs as they talked. Iollan had scouted out the place I described from the necromancer's memory.

"There's an old church there. It's ruins now. Has some graffiti warning the place is haunted. But there are very old trees around it, so traveling in and from there will be simple."

"More tree travel? Oh joy," Levi said, pulling up a seat. "I got the supplies you asked for, though I had to arm-wrestle Rosie for some of them." He winked at me and nudged a duffel bag he'd set down behind Harper's chair.

"You sure you want to come?" I asked him around a mouthful of toast. As much as I valued his company, I wasn't sure how I felt putting my friend in danger and asking him to leave his pregnant wife. Junebug was an adult, so she understood risks, but the baby inside her wouldn't know that their dad was dead because of something I asked him to do that was important to me.

"I'm not letting my brother and my best friends go raise a vampire without me. Besides, Alek's not bad for a Justice. I'd miss him," Levi said. "Y'all are my ride or die."

"More riding, no dying," I muttered as I finished my meal. "All right, let's go wake up mommy dearest."

In my head when I thought of abandoned churches in the wilderness, I supposed I had a very Western medieval idea of such formed from decades of watching movies. But nobody had built a cathedral in the Frank. Instead we stumbled out of the trees, four of us still a little green around the mouth from what Harper had dubbed "tree-coaster" travel, and found ourselves standing in front of a crumbling brick and cedar rectangle that was more cabin than cathedral. The roof was mostly gone, collapsed inward in parts and clearly salvaged and taken away from other parts. The northern wall was partially collapsed also, the bricks bending inward as though a stiff breeze could topple them at any moment. The doors on the west end were missing, shafts of late afternoon sunlight illuminating an interior overgrown with moss and ferns and a few brave chokecherry saplings. Only a large brick arch remained where the doors would have hung.

"I will wait and keep watch here," Iollan said. The big druid turned and walked over to lean against the thick trunk of a pine.

"Thanks," I said as I walked into the dubious shade of the archway.

"Should I keep watch with you?" Ezee hesitated in the doorway, looking back over his shoulder at his husband. I didn't see Iollan's response, but something passed between the two of them, and Ezee shrugged with a tiny smile on his face before following me into the building.

"You sure this is the place?" Levi asked as we picked our way over the rubble and into the shadowed interior.

"Under the altar," I said, hoping that the necromancer's memory wasn't leading us astray. There wasn't time to play "find the crypt" if this wasn't the place.

"At least that's still standing," Harper said, scrambling through some ferns and over a pile of fallen, rotting wood toward the back of the rectangle.

Coming up behind her, I skidded to down the pile and came to a halt in front of a huge stone box. The dais it had been set on was just a larger square of stone. Nothing grew on the dais or the altar, not even a hint of moss or lichen.

"Creepy," Levi said, reaching out to poke the stone as though it would somehow come to life and bite him.

"Yes, creepy, so definitely touch it first thing," Ezee said, swatting at his brother's arm.

"So Li—she's in that?" Harper asked, starting to say Lilith's name but then avoiding it, as though the mere word would summon her. "There's no smell of death or anything here."

"It doesn't smell like anything at all right here," Levi said.

I sniffed too, even though I lacked shifter senses. But they were right. The smell of loam and pine and summer blooming things filling the air with pollen and life that had been so prevalent outside was missing here. The air was sterile-feeling, dry in my mouth and nose. Tiny hairs on my neck lifted.

"Right place," I said. I moved around the altar, looking for the small symbols that should be carved in the stone slab.

"How do we open it?" Levi stage-whispered to Ezee and Harper.

"Shh, she's working on that, obviously."

"Relax. She's not in the altar," I said. I smiled as I found the carving right where the necromancer's memories said it was. A beam of sunlight wavered over them, illuminating nine marks in the stone that felt rough beneath my fingers as I touched them gently. A bird, a sword, a diamond, a heart with a smaller heart shape inside, a few I couldn't really guess at or see clearly in the wavering late summer sunlight. The sun was setting and would be gone in an hour. Time was running out.

"But I thought you said—" Levi started to say, but the other two hushed him.

"How do we get it open? Lift?" Ezee asked as Levi subsided with a roll of his eyes.

"Blood," I said, summoning magic to form a claw on my right index finger. "Vampires, remember? Blood to open, blood to summon, blood to awaken." The words from the tome resonated in my brain as well as in the church, taking on weight as I spoke them.

"Yeah I am definitely creeped out now," Harper muttered.

My friends all backed away as I pricked my left palm with the magic claw. A drop of blood welled from the tiny wound almost before I felt the sting.

"Here goes nothing," I said, and I pressed my hand to the symbols, running the bloody skin over each in turn.

Without sound or warning, the huge stone altar sank into the dais, dropping away into darkness as though it had never been. A cool breeze shivered over us as air, dusty and long-undisturbed, rushed from the opening in the altar. Blue lights blinked into existence inside as I peered over the edge. The lights were along a set of narrow stairs spiraling down into whispering darkness. A feeling of expectation pressed against me. Something waited below, I felt it in my bones, in my primal brain screaming that this was a terrible idea.

"Tell me we are not going down there," Ezee said with a snarl. His eyes had a golden glow to their depths that I saw mirrored in Levi's.

"I could do this part alone," I said. I had no idea what waited below. The book had been a little thin on description there.

"Like hell. Ladies first, I guess," Harper said, meeting my gaze with a forced grin as she walked forward. She drew the Alpha and Omega, the blade's surface shimmering faintly blue in a way that was more than just a reflection of the light from below.

"Sorceress first," I said, closing my fist around my sore palm. I wasn't done bleeding, if what I'd read was correct, but at least this small wound had already closed. We were here to save Alek and he was my mate. Captured because of me. My responsibility.

With a deep breath and a braver face than I felt, I moved onto the first step. Then the second. My magic flooded my veins as my skin crawled, but I kept walking, down, and down, and down, into the waiting dark below.

9

The stairs widened into a long stone spiral downward, with open air to the left and only winking blue light to guide us. I summoned a ball of light into my hand, ready to unleash it as more than just light if needed, but the darkness hardly retreated, as though my light was hitting a wall. The feeling of menace grew as we descended, but the air remained creepily still and silent. The only sounds were the slight scuff of our shoes and the too-loud-seeming huff of our breath.

"I smell water," Harper murmured from behind me. Ezee and Levi both grunted in what I assumed was agreement.

A few stairs farther down I caught the scent as the

air turned damper and a degree cooler. The steps ended another five below into a circular room paved with small white stones. There was a doorway immediately to the right of the steps opening into a very short corridor with a heavy metal and wood door at the end. The blue lights encircled the door, gleaming on the pristine silvery filigree and polished steel bars crisscrossing its surface. The corridor was only just wide enough for one of us to go at a time.

"I have so much more empathy for my D&D characters now," Levi said.

"This is probably a lot more fun when you have actual saving throws," Ezee agreed.

"And a proper rogue to check for traps," Harper added.

I decided not to be insulted by that last one. "I have a lot more hit points than your average player character sorceress," I said as I cautiously stepped into the corridor. The stone floor didn't fall away, nor was I impaled by spears or spiked chains or poison darts or whatever else my imagination was conjuring from a lifetime of inventing places just like this for games.

Taking a deep breath, I walked up to the door. This part had no instruction manual. Robert Loughlin, the necromancer, hadn't been able to open the stairway. He'd tried a bunch of different kinds of blood but nothing had had much effect. The ritual Alek and I had interrupted to raise a monster had been his latest, and last, attempt to find something with blood powerful enough to work. Apparently controlling Ishimaru had backfired, because the necromantic magic tainted the vampire's blood, rendering it useless for this purpose.

Dragon sorceress blood was just peachy, apparently. As I'd suspected it would be. I mean, if a drop of my blood was strong enough to build a ward to keep me out, I figured more would be able to get me in here. Not that I'd really had a Plan B other than huff and puff and blow the house down.

The door was locked. I couldn't even find a handle or anything that looked like a catch or keyhole. The others stayed out of the corridor but called out helpful advice as I felt around the door.

"Bleed on it?"

"Speak 'Friend' and enter?"

"Open Sesame?"

"With friends like these," I muttered, but I was smiling anyway. Blood was the most likely solution, so

I used magic to cut myself again and smeared my palm across the door, ready to leap back if needed.

Nothing happened.

"Not blood then I guess?" Harper said as she leaned into the corridor. "No keyhole or anything?"

"No," I said as I held my stinging hand to my chest, careful not to smear blood on my teeshirt. "Stand back—we're going with Plan B."

"What's Plan B?" Levi stage-whispered to the others.

"Throw magic at it and hope for the best," I said as I backed up the corridor.

"Please don't bury us down here," Ezee said. "Not that I don't have total trust in you, but this is not how I want to die."

"Nobody is dying today," I said with more confidence than I felt. I knew on a surface level that I should take more time and try to figure out the door, but I was tired. I was tired of obstacles, of never having all the answers, and this door was about to feel my frustration.

Magic flowed into my hands even as I thought of it, the power in my veins crackling as static along my arms. Purple sparks dripped from my skin. I took a deep breath and focused on the door. I had no idea what lay on the other side, but hopefully it wasn't super squishy. I focused power in front of my hands, reveling in the flow of magic and how simple it was to conjure this much. It was as though my weeks of weakness, injury, and starvation had never happened, at least magically speaking. A tiny voice in the back of my head worried about how easy this was, but I quieted it. Those fears were for later. Much *much* later, when everyone I loved was home and safe and I had the luxury of worrying about morals and power-spikes.

"Knock, knock," I said as I thrust my hands forward, sending the power in a wave at the door. I must have sent far more than I felt like I was, because the door blew backward like a leaf in a strong wind and crashed down with a whooshing smash onto the stones behind it. I expected recoil but felt none, just a slight breeze as the air changed and moved in response to the door flying backward and falling over.

Silence followed as I reined in my power and we all held our breaths waiting for who knew what. Silence. A soft golden light illuminated a room beyond the fallen door, glimmering on what looked like water.

I glanced at my friends and they gave me nods of

encouragement. Even Levi looked impressed by how easily I'd taken out the heavy, fancy door. One by one we crept down the corridor and through the opening I'd made.

To the left was a deep, still pool of water that stretched into darkness beyond where the light could reach. The cavern, for that was what it felt like, was about the size of the great hall at the Den from what I could tell, though the darkness and water to the left might have gone on for who knew how long since darkness hid them in that direction. The white marble flooring led up to another dais built of gold and white marble. On the dais was a table, or perhaps a bed, encased in shimmering crystal, cut into prisms that caught the golden light and tossed back tiny glints of rainbow. The light fixtures were two naked human statues, one male, one female, carved in a classical style and holding large gold balls from which the glow emanated.

I walked carefully along the edge of the water toward the dais, stopping short of it by a couple of feet. Even this close I couldn't see inside the crystal dome very well, but I made out the form of a body lying on dark bedding. Lilith, I presumed.

"There's no breeze," Ezee said as he came up beside me.

"No," I said, distracted as I searched the necromancer's memories again. I needed to set up the circle that would hold her until the bargain could be struck before I attempted to wake her up.

"So why is the lake moving?" Levi said, a note of alarm creeping into his voice with a growl.

That pulled me from my thoughts right quick. Levi shifted into his wolverine as we all backed away from the now-rippling waters. Nothing good ever came out of dark water in a crypt, and that was true in life as well as gaming I imagined. We were about to find out.

Harper stepped in front of us, brandishing the brightly glowing Alpha and Omega. Ezee shifted into a coyote as two large grey-green tentacles surged from the water and wrapped around Harper's legs, yanking her from her feet before any of us could react.

I summoned fire but held it back at the last second, realizing I couldn't be sure I wouldn't hit my friend. Harper gave a mighty yell as she was pulled under the water and swung the blade. I formed blades of power in my hands and rushed in after her.

Cold hit me like a truck to the face—if the truck

was made of dry ice, the surface of Mars, and the worst Idaho winter weather you've ever made the mistake of going out in with only pajamas on for a quick look at the mailbox. I plunged in above my head as I stepped from stone to nothing, air smashing out of my lungs.

I don't need to breathe, I reminded myself. Air was optional. I forced my eyes open. Magic surged in my veins, warming me, thrusting back the paralyzing cold. I swam toward a faint blue light, hoping that was Harper and not just the sword. A tentacle smashed into my side, and I lashed out with magic, severing it with purple fire that boiled and hissed in the water. I kicked hard, following the trail of inky blood and the blue glow. As I swam down I refocused my magic, turning the purple fire blades to ropes instead, visualizing lifelines extending and hooking.

A huge grey-green body, like a giant worm, reared up from below, writhing. I kicked off its powerful coils as the waves from its body churned the water. Something grabbed my arm. I stopped myself short of blasting it with magic as Harper's face appeared in front of me, her eyes open, her skin pale in the light of the blade still clutched in her right hand. The body of the monster churned away, falling down, or what I assumed was down, into dark depths. I wasn't sure what was up, but it was clear from Harper's desperate expression that she was out of air. I wrapped my arms around her, careful of the sword, and threw the power ropes in what I hoped was an upward direction. They hooked onto something and I used the magic lines to drag us upward.

We shot out of the water and nearly hit the cavern ceiling. I managed to cushion that with a bubble of magic at the last moment. Envisioning us light as feathers, I used magic to lower us slowly to where a very unhappy and wet pair of shifters waited. Ezee and Levi shifted back to their human bodies as we landed. Harper lay on her back, gasping, as I let her go and drew in a deep, relieved breath.

"That was too... many... teeth..." Harper wheezed out.

I decided I could spare some magic to dry us all off and did so, summoning a hot wind that swirled around me and then Harper, and finally Ezee and Levi.

"Thanks," Harper said.

"That's a lot of juice you are using," Ezee said, a speculative and concerned look tightening his jaw and narrowing his eyes.

"I've got plenty," I said. I walked to where Levi had dropped the small duffel bag and opened it. Hopefully nothing else ugly would come out of the lake, because I still had a lot to do and I would need to concentrate to do it. Ritual magic was not my strong suit.

"That's not concerning you a little?" Ezee pressed as Levi helped Harper to her feet.

"I'm going to worry about that later," I assured him. There was no time to be concerned. I had a vampire to wake up.

What felt like too long later, but was less than three hours if Ezee's phone was correct, I was as ready as I was going to get. I'd drawn the complex circles around the dais, managing to get them perfect even with three people watching me and arguing about if it was "klaatu barada nikto" or "clatto verata necto" or maybe "klaatu verata nicto" instead. I almost told them to shut up, but I knew this was how we all handled pressure. I could likely have accomplished this whole bit on my own, but I'd be sadder and lonelier for it. Or maybe spending the night in a lake monster's stomach—after all, Harper had killed it, not I.

All that was left was to use my blood to infuse the circles with power and awaken Lilith.

"I'll feel better if you all back up to the corridor at least. Please," I added.

The tension must have finally gotten to them, too, because none of the three argued with me.

"Sure you don't want the sword?" Harper asked.

"No, keep it. If this goes really poorly, it'll be good to have you at my back." I smiled at her with more confidence than I felt.

Harper joined the twins at the mouth of the corridor, standing by the fallen door. They had my back. I turned and faced the dais and the crystal dome. Time to find out if quality over quantity held for blood rituals also.

Robert Loughlin had spent his whole life studying death in a bid to outrun it. I had walled off his mind-ghost in my head before starting this, not wanting to deal with his ego, and maybe also a little out of pity. His ghost shouldn't have to witness me doing something he'd dreamed of and worked decades for. I was glad the actual magic involved wasn't necromantic in nature for the most part, because it still made my skin crawl even touching the memories of that sickly-sweet, rotten power. Vampires might be undead in their way, but whatever they were was tied more to life than death. I could tell that from the feel of them alone.

I stood at the edge of the outermost circle and summoned a magic claw again. This time I had to cut pretty deep into my arm. I made the cut in the meat of my forearm instead of my palm this time, using magic and my willpower to direct the blood into the lines of chalk. I had a feeling when Walmart sold these packs of sidewalk chalk that the advertising didn't say anything about how great they were at drawing arcane symbols on marble crypt flooring, but it had worked out well. Blood and magic surged from me, leaving me dizzy.

Kneeling down to steady myself, I kept the stream of power flowing. The lines I'd draw flared to life with faint red flames, and the blood flowing from my arm spread out along them with impossible volume. When every line on each of the three circles was illuminated, I cut the power, tying it off in my mind. The magic held.

Step one was finished.

Now the fun part. I curled my right hand over the still-leaking wound in my arm, gathering blood along with my magic.

"Lilith, I call you," I said in Japanese. This part was from Ishimaru, what he'd told the necromancer when he was enslaved before the necromantic magic degraded his body too far for him to speak in coherent sentences any longer. He'd told the necromancer under duress, so it was basically wish and prayer that the information was good.

"Lilith, I call you," I said again, this time in Greek. I repeated the phrase, or the equivalent translation of it, seven more times after that, each time in a different language. A couple of the languages I didn't even know, but my innate gift with such things let me know I was saying it correctly.

My hand was full and overflowing with blood by the time I finished. I cast the handful in a wide arc. Blood rained down onto the crystal dome. It shattered with a musical note, the shards dissolving into mist before they hit the figure enshrined within.

The remaining blood on my arm and hand were pulled through the air toward the platform, almost tugging me with it before I braced my feet and cut off the flow from my own wound. Stifled gasps sounded behind me, but I kept my gaze on the dais. My innate healing magic kicked in, closing the gash I'd made and sealing away my blood. Glancing down at my feet, I realized how perilously close I'd come to crossing the outer circle. The toe of my boot almost touched the glowing circle. A centimeter more and I would have wrecked it.

"You are not one of mine," came a gentle, melodic voice in perfect English.

I looked up and into the face of the Mother of All Vampires.

10

Lilith sat on the edge of the platform, looking like an actress or a model arrayed for a photoshoot more than a vampire awakened after nearly a century of magic sleep. She was wearing a dark purple dressing gown straight out of a Jane Austen movie, and little else from what I could see. Her skin was a very light golden-hued brown, which shouldn't have surprised me, but I still thought of vampires as super-pale creatures of darkness, I guess. Her hair fell in rich brown waves over her shoulders and drifted across her nearly revealed full breasts, but it was her glinting golden eyes and the deceptively mild smile on her wide red lips that drew my attention. Her tone had been questioning, and her eyebrows were raised as though she expected some kind of answer.

"No," I said, gathering my wits. "I'm here about one of your children though. In a way."

Lilith rose and tried to step off the dais. She hissed and pulled back as the inner circle flared with power, but thankfully held.

"This is unnecessary," she said. She had none of the stillness I'd come to associate with vampires. Whatever she was, I had a feeling she was either way better at pretending to be alive than her children, or perhaps she was not undead at all.

"Better safe than sorry. Someone once told me never to trust a vampire, and I've learned the hard way to listen to that advice," I said. So many questions raced through my head. The first was why had her children locked her away down here? She'd been here since the eighteen hundreds, if the necromancer's information was correct.

"It's almost eleven," Ezee said very quietly in an apologetic tone behind me. I had told him to warn me when it got to the eleventh hour, literally and figuratively.

"Now there is one I could work with," Lilith said,

smiling at Ezee. "Come here, gorgeous."

"He's taken," Levi said.

"We're all taken," Harper said.

"Have you ever truly been taken, fox? I think not from your reaction to me."

"Okay, hey, nobody is doing any taking," I said before I had to stop Harper from running the Mother of All Vampires through with a magic sword.

"Then why wake me up?" Lilith's attention snapped back to me, and I almost took a step back from the power of her gaze. Her question and Ezee's warning snapped me out of my thoughts. We were here for one reason, and curiosity about anything else just might kill the only cat that truly mattered to me.

"It's a long story, but the short version is that Noah Grey," —I saw from the lift of her chin that she knew that name— "is holding my mate hostage until I give him something he wants. Which I don't have to give him. So instead you and I are going to make a deal. Your freedom for my mate's freedom."

Lilith studied me a long moment and then her smile returned, but this time it touched her eyes. "You think I can, what? Snap my fingers and order Noah to hand over your mate?" She snapped her fingers, and I managed not to flinch. Go me.

"Yes," I said, spreading my hands. The plan did sound a bit thin when put that way, but desperate times and desperate measures. It had taken nine of them to lock her away down here, so I was going on the assumption that any single vampire kid of hers was likely way less powerful than Mom.

"All right," she said. "I agree. I will make this bargain. I will order my son to hand over your mate. You will set me free."

I motioned for my friends to quiet as they all started to object to this oversimplification of things. This wasn't my first rodeo with beings who stuck to the letter of agreements and not the spirit.

"No. You will promise to do everything in your power to get my mate, Aleksei Kirov, back from your son, Noah Grey. You will also agree to leave me and mine alone afterward and to never set foot in Wylde, Idaho, or the surrounding area ever again. That is the bargain." Even as I said the words I knew there were likely holes in this I wasn't seeing, but I was tired and midnight was coming on fast. At least this would hopefully keep vampires out of my home. We had enough problems.

Lilith shrugged, her robe slipping and threatening to fall off her statuesque shoulders. Levi made a strangled sound behind me.

"If you removed the metal from your face, I'd have you, glutton. I like the fierce ones."

"Get bent," Levi said.

"Do you agree to the bargain or not? Or do you want to add something?" I said, trying to keep the desperation from my voice.

"Let me guess, there's a 'stroke of midnight' timeline on this? Noah always had a flair for drama." Lilith took my glower as her answer. "Very well, I agree. If you free me, I will do all in my power to free your mate, this Aleksei, and you can trust I have no desire to return to this place. You and yours are safe from me. I so swear and all that bother."

"Wait, you just agreed? Without any stipulations other than freeing you?" I couldn't quite believe it.

"Your terms are acceptable. I agree. Free me." Lilith waved an imperious hand.

I risked a look behind me. Ezee looked unhappy but he nodded. Levi was suspiciously flushed and chewing furiously on a lip piercing, but he, too, met my eye and gave a single shoulder shrug. Harper flexed her hand on the hilt of the Alpha and Omega where she'd resheathed it at her waist, but she nodded after a moment.

"She's gonna love the tree-coaster," Harper said with a wan smile.

"Tree... coaster?" Lilith asked.

"We'll get to that," I said. I stepped up to the line of chalk again. I'd done stupider things for love. Maybe.

"Lilith, I accept the bargain. Be freed." I added the last part because it felt like I should. Noah wasn't the only one who could do drama. Then I smeared my boot across the line. The power in the chalk and blood circles snapped apart with an audible pop and the red light died away.

Lilith descended from the dais like a queen and it was all I could do to hold my ground. She had two or three inches on my height and was easily half again my weight, especially in my current post-captivity state, but her charismatic presence and the feeling of something old and powerful lurking behind the movie-star façade were truly intimidating. My lizard brain recognized the predator. All the things my ancestors had feared went bump in the night were embodied in this beautiful woman, and my subconscious knew it. But I wasn't a rabbit or a lizard.

So I stood still under her scrutiny for a moment, and then deliberately turned my back, even though every instinct in my body screamed obscenities at me for doing so.

"Let's go get Alek," I said. I didn't look behind to see if she followed, but from my friends faces, she did.

"Aren't you curious what year it is?" Levi asked her as we made our way up the steps.

"I am used to awakening in strange eras," Lilith said, her voice a caress in the dim stairwell. "Live long enough and you learn there is a time and place for such things. But what is this tree-coaster? This I have never heard of."

Upon exiting the chapel we learned two things. First, even Lilith the Mother of All Vampires found Iollan the druid too intimidating to tease, and second, that she was really, really excited about tree travel.

"That was amazing!" Lilith was laughing, a deep, melodic laugh that shook her ample chest and shoulders and made me feel even queasier as we were pushed from the tree by druidic magic.

"She's not okay," Harper muttered from where she'd rushed off to the side to vomit. She wiped her mouth with the hem of her teeshirt.

"I get so few new experiences, little fox," Lilith said, looking around the silent park with interest. "If you survive a century or two, you will see the value in newness and excitement again."

"How do you know I'm not already that old?" Harper said with a glare.

Lilith just laughed again.

"Where are we?" I swallowed more bile and looked at Iollan. Time was running thin. This stand of old trees looked like any other to me, and though the streets were lit, I didn't know Seattle well enough to guess how close we were to the Archivist's warehouse.

"You can't smell the sound?" Ezee asked.

"All I can smell right now is my own stomach acid," I said.

"We are not far," Iollan assured me.

Ezee knew the way from here, so the druid stayed behind to keep watch on our exit. I wasn't sure what state Alek would be in, so as much as I wished I could have left everyone but Lilith safely behind me, if Alek needed help, I couldn't exactly carry him on my own. Which meant that Ezee, Levi, and Harper all came along.

It took nearly twenty minutes to walk to where the warehouse loomed along the quiet waterfront. The city felt subdued, though we'd seen plenty of people still going about their oblivious lives. I reminded myself it wasn't anything sinister, but normal for close to midnight on a weekday, and work night, for most denizens. Lilith was barefoot, but she said nothing about it, so none of us brought it up. Wasn't like anyone was keen to carry her. After the apparent exhilaration of the tree-coaster, she was surprisingly subdued as we walked, staring around her with wide eyes and raised brows.

I wondered if she was hungry after sleeping that long, but she didn't bring that up either, and I wasn't about to offer anything. It was enough that she was holding to our bargain so far. My heart started beating faster as we turned down a familiar street and approached the warehouse. Alek was so close now. This plan had to work. As terrifying as it was to place my hopes on Lilith, the plot was in motion, and there wasn't anything I could do for the moment but hope.

Noah Grey was standing where he had been the night before, waiting expectantly on the far side of the bright white line forming a broad circle around his property. The line keeping me out. Not for much longer, I hoped.

It was gratifying to see the recognition and then fear in his face as we approached. Noah's lips drew back in a hiss, baring his fangs as Lilith gave him a little wave. I motioned for Harper and the twins to stay back, then walked with Lilith up to the line.

"Did you miss me?" Lilith stepped over the line and brushed a lock of hair off the Archivist's forehead. He stepped back with inhuman speed and turned his glare on me.

"You don't know what you've done," Noah said.

"Our bargain, Lilith," I reminded her as I laid my fingers against the magical barrier. It tingled under my hand, pushing back on me but not repelling me yet.

"The sorceress would like her mate back," Lilith said. "Hand him over." A note of sharpened steel slid below the velvet of her voice.

Noah looked at her, then back at me, then at her again. Slowly he shook his head.

My heart danced on a knife edge. If she couldn't make Noah give Alek back, I was out of plans and Alek would now be at the mercy of two vampires.

"That was not a request, child," Lilith said, her voice turning to smoke and a promise of pain.

"I cannot give her what I do not have," Noah said, speaking the words as though they hurt him. There was more expression on the vampire's face than I'd ever seen, fear and pain warring with something I couldn't name. Relief? Amusement? It was hard to tell in the dim light.

"Where is he?" I said, controlling my urge to start fireballing the planet if that was what it took to bring down this stupid ward so I could find out how slowly a vampire could die for good.

"I had an interesting talk with Ainsley's remains," Noah said, his eyes flicking to Lilith as she folded her arms beneath her breasts and tapped on bare foot in mock impatience. "It seemed strange to me that you would have Samir's heart close, and then your words yesterday, they felt… off. A lie but not a lie. Like when you told me how you killed the necromancer."

"Where. Is. Alek?" I laid my other palm against the ward, the tingling increasing to almost-pain as I pressed on it.

"I know you love your theatrics, but get to the point. I am hungry and could use a nice bath," Lilith said.

"I realized what had changed, in the feel of the world. You proved me right, Jade Crow. You could not be trusted. You have eaten Samir's heart, so whatever you showed up here tonight with, it would not be what I wanted. I decided it would be too dangerous to keep Alek here any longer and there was someone else who would pay a great deal for him."

"You fucking bastard," I said, slamming my hands into the barrier. My feet skidded backward as the barrier rebounded into me. "You gave him to the First?"

"I did. This morning after I realized you could not and would not uphold our bargain. He is not mine to give, therefore, no matter how much Lilith commands me, I cannot obey."

Power howled through me, wind rising from nowhere and lifting leaves and debris and small bits of gravel into the air. The ground started to shake and I heard the sound of waves crashing into shore, though that might have been the blood and rage in my ears.

"Jade?" Harper's concerned tone from behind me

made me pull the power back a notch.

"Samir is dead? Interesting," Lilith said. She looked at me and spread her hands wide. "I have done what is in my power to do. I cannot get your mate back from my son, since he no longer has him."

"You gave him to the First?" I repeated, trying to wrap my head around it. Yesterday, Alek had been here. Today, he was gone, in the hands of an enemy whose face I didn't even know, much less what the First's true plans for Alek or Wylde even were.

"I do not think he wants Alek dead, if that is any consolation," Noah said.

"Can you get him back?" I asked, fighting to rein in the magic flooding me.

"Answer her," Lilith said, her voice sharp again.

"No," Noah said after a long moment where he appeared to consider. "I have nothing of more value to trade, nor the resources to take on the First and an army of shifters directly."

Which he had known, the bastard. The fucking slimy undead pustule of a dickpickle bastard.

"That's why you did it," I hissed. The First was already my problem on account of what he was doing to my town. Now Noah had effectively made it super personal, redirecting me from him to the First. In his twisted mind, it was better for me to focus on a different enemy, buying Noah time to play ten dimensional chess with me later, or whatever it was he did like a poisonous old spider in a moldering web.

But it would only save him for now. My business with the vampire wasn't over. Lilith had asked for no concessions to protect her children from me. I hoped that she would make his un-life hell enough in the meantime.

"Yes. This ward will not stand forever." Noah shrugged, his inhuman movements back in place. "You do not know what you have done," he repeated, looking again at Lilith and then back to me. "I would have thought eating Samir's heart was the worst mistake you've made, but…" he trailed off with a shake of his head.

"Mistakes I've made? Worry about your own, vampire." I could barely get the words out. "If Lilith doesn't end you, Archivist, I will. Not today. Not tomorrow even. But you will never be able to stop looking over your shoulder, and some day, I will be there."

"What does the First look like? Where is he?" Ezee asked, coming up beside me.

Lilith nodded at Noah, her eyebrow raised.

"I dealt with his shifter minions only. Alek was handed over nearly where you stand now."

Rage spun a whirlwind of power around me at those words, and only Ezee's firm grip on my arm stopped me from unleashing uselessly on the barrier. I didn't have to ask to know that Noah had likely requested no face to face on purpose. He'd known I would be back.

"Tell him to take down the ward," I said to Lilith, though I had a feeling already that she would refuse.

She did, with a polite shake of her head. "No, I have far too much I need to discuss with Noah before you rip him limb from limb. I think it best you stay where you are. Our bargain is fulfilled."

"I bet that won't keep me out," Harper said, stepping up beside me. She had the Alpha and Omega in her hand. "Or maybe it'll take out the ward."

"Do we kill him or keep him alive to talk?" Levi said, coming up with Ezee on the other side of me. The words ended in a snarl that left no question which he was voting for.

"He's the Archivist," Ezee said. "He knows more about the First than he's telling us."

"That was not part of the agreement; I have done

everything in my power," Lilith said, "I have need of Noah, so I'm afraid if any of you cross that line, I shall be forced to do something unpleasant."

"Maybe she's bluffing," Harper said, looking at me with hard, determined eyes.

For a moment, I truly considered it, but I was stuck on this side and there was no guarantee that even if Harper managed to kill Noah that the ward would drop. We had no idea what Lilith was capable of, but underestimating her could prove fatal. A vision of my friends fighting and dying on the other side of an impenetrable ward flashed across my brain. I wasn't losing anyone else, not like this.

"There will be a reckoning," I said, even as I shook my head at Harper and pushed her gently back. Ezee laid a hand on Levi's arm and did the same.

"I am hungry and my feet are cold. Further conversation will get us nothing we need. Your mate is with the First. Go deal with him. Leave what is mine to me." Lilith made a shooing motion with one hand as she stepped forward to settle the other on Noah's shoulder.

The Archivist's frightened look was the tiniest consolation prize in the Universe. There was nothing I could do or say, though I had a few more choice words and final desperate questions that went ignored as Lilith and Noah went up the steps and disappeared through the heavy metal door, leaving us standing in the empty parking lot, only the warm wind my raging power had conjured swirling around us.

I'd lost the gamble.

Alek was gone.

Alek

The first time Alek awakened, he was too injured to move. The world was narrowed to pain and the smell of antiseptic fluids. His mind worked, even if his body wanted nothing to do with the waking world.

Jade. Her face, terrified and spattered with blood, his or hers or both, Alek was not sure. Jade. She could not hear him, but he said the words anyway. Her name. That he loved her.

And then, his memory in slow motion from the trauma and adrenaline, he watched as she pushed her necklace into her mouth. Her beautiful, dark eyes widening. A hum of power rising.

Then her hair flying forward, hitting him in a wet wave. Her eyes, dark and full of love and desperation and promises, going dull and empty as he spat bone and blood from his mouth still roaring her name.

Her name was on his chapped lips the second time he awoke. His body was less filled with razors, his muscles sluggishly responding as he tested and flexed them. The hospital-like smells were gone, replaced with the scent of human bodies, Dial soap, and faint industrial smells beneath that. Grease, dust, iron rusting in the faint damp. There was water nearby as well, clean enough smelling, though the fluoride he detected said it came from pipes, likely in a city. Not Idaho, was his guess. There was little public water fluoridation there. He was somewhere else.

Alek opened his eyes and let them adjust to the bright light. There was a stone ceiling overhead. Bars to the left and right of him. Front and behind as well. He was laying on the floor of a cage; the softness beneath him was a foam mattress. He was naked, his body a crisscrossed pockmarked mass of healing wounds. Detecting no sounds of humans and seeing nothing in the dim room beyond the industrial lights pointed his way, Alek decided it was safe to rise. If he could. Muscles protesting, Alek got slowly to his feet. There was a jug of water next to his bedding. Thirst won over caution, and he drank deep. He needed his strength if he was to escape this and find Jade.

A bullet through the brain would not kill his mate, only slow her down for a little while. Alek bared his teeth at the thought, wishing there were someone around here to give him answers or, barring those, to shed some blood in recompense for this catastrophe.

Half the jug gone, Alek set it down and paced the cage, testing every bar for weakness. There was a toilet apparently plumbed into the floor on one side of his cage, the only thing in it aside from the foam pad he had been sleeping on. The toilet was porcelain and had all the extra parts removed down to its bare functioning. The lights were hot and bright, pointing directly into his cage from all sides, occluding whatever was beyond from even his keen vision.

Whatever the alloy was, it held against his progressively angrier and angrier yanks and pulls. He could identify no door or hinge, and the bars were too close together for him to squeeze through, even in his thinner state. The metal groaned but hardly bent a centimeter. He shifted, throwing the full might of his tiger into the bars. He won new bruises for his efforts and little else.

"Are you quite satisfied?" a soft voice asked.

Alek growled as a man walked out of the shadows.

He shifted to human, stepping away from the bars a pace. The man, who smelled of soap and wool and nothing human at all, had no detectible heart beat and his movements were stiff but too fast to be mortal. As he stepped fully into the light, Alek's nostrils flared and he snarled. He knew this man.

Brown hair and flat silver eyes, an angular face that hid a predatory expression even as he forced a small smile. The vampire looked small and weak, but Alek was in the cage, and he recognized a dangerous creature when he saw one. They had never formally met, but Alek knew his name.

"Noah Grey," he said. "Where is Jade?"

"How did I know that would be your first question?" The vampire chuckled, the sound grating in the silence. No breath moved his chest, no blood through his veins, no heartbeat. "She is healing elsewhere."

Alek was unsure if he would know if the vampire lied to him, and the thought fueled his rising anger. "Why have you done this?" The vampire wanted Samir's heart, that much was clear. He had been behind the mage in the Frank, and so in Alek's mind was responsible for Trueheart and the others who had died from that mage's evil experiments. He growled as the vampire took a while to answer.

"I did not do this," Noah said, waving a hand to indicate Alek's scarred body. "But we must make do with what we have, no? If Jade gives me what I want, this little stay here will be but a moment in your very long lives together."

A lifetime of living with people who could read every heartbeat, micro-expression, and breath kept Alek from reacting. The image of Jade's blood-soaked face as she pushed her D20 into her mouth filled his mind, but he brushed it away. Even if she had it to give, Jade would never hand over Samir's heart to the vampire. Hopefully.

A small voice in his mind whispered that was not true. She had eaten it to save him; the love and desperation in her eyes before the light went out affirmed that in ways no words ever would. Samir's heart was no longer hers to give, not without giving her own up.

Alek was not sure Jade would see how poor a trade that was. Which left one solution. He had to get out here before it became an issue.

"I know where the heart is," Alek said, pitching his voice low and calm.

Noah laughed. "I imagine you do. Let me guess, you will tell me if I set you free?" The words were accompanied by no change in expression despite the mirth in them, as though the vampire was not bothering to pretend to humanity or life.

"Why not?"

"It may come to that," Noah said, his voice going somber. "But you are worth more to me this way, for now."

It was clear by "that" the vampire meant torturing the answer out of Alek or some similar plan. Alek knew they would find he did not break so easily. He would bash his brains out upon these bars before he betrayed Jade that way. Torture only truly worked in movies.

"Come closer," he growled to the vampire. "Perhaps we can work this out between us." Alek stepped close to the bars again, flexing his hands.

The vampire did not flinch, exactly, but he did move away, stepping back into the shadows. "Enjoy your stay with us," Noah said as he left, his steps as silent going as they had been entering.

This time Alek heard the door close, the sound

traveling around the space until he had some idea of the size of the room. Large. Mostly empty. Electricity hummed in the light cords. His breathing rasped. Alek sat down to wait and plan.

The first time a human pushed a protein shake bottle through the bars, Alek did nothing. He waited until the two men backed away before picking up the bottle from the ground. He waited until they were gone to drink it, then carefully set the empty bottle back on the other side of the bars. One of the men had a cattle prod, which amused Alek. He could take so much more pain than that would offer. But he still had no idea how to open the cage. So he waited, watching, timing each visit, looking for weakness or change.

The next time someone came, there were three of them. They ordered him to put the empty water jug at the bars and step back. Alek complied, not bothering to ask these minions questions. They had a bought-and-paid for look about them with their identical tailored suits and haircuts. They even smelled of the same soap and aftershave. Company men. It did not surprise him that the vampire employed such. Familiar smells and looks would be soothing to someone with heightened senses, and would promote a sense of order for the humans to feel more comfortable around a predator. They filled his water jug from one they had brought with them. Alek watched this process with interest, for it brought two of them close to the bars, one having to reach through to steady the jug while the other aimed the spout on the refill.

They fed him random things. Protein shakes in little bottles. A package of pre-cut apples. A string of salty sausages. The men were clearly under a "no conversation" rule; they did not even talk amongst themselves, much less to respond to the easy questions Alek tried to tempt them with from time to time.

It was always the same two or three. Alek assigned them names based on their looks and mannerisms. Big was the one who acted more in charge, always holding the cattle prod and ordering the other two with gestures to do whatever they had come to do. Sandy was the blond who walked like his hips were out of alignment. They were the main two, the third man came only when the water needed refilling. Alek dubbed him Meat, because he was the one who reached through the cage, and Alek had plans for him.

He debated breaking the toilet to see if they would come in and fix it, but had the feeling that should be a last resort. It would not shock him if they left it broken and started hosing him down or some nonsense, so that plan went to the back of his mind. He was underfed but not uncomfortable in the cage. It was large enough he could shift and pace, or stretch out to sleep, which he did in short bursts to keep his strength up. The lights were constant, no way to measure time except in the brief visits of his captors. The vampire did not return for conversation, despite Alek's many requests to the minions to bring him.

The water jug sat at the edge of the cage, empty. Alek knelt on his foam pad, his head down, eyes closed. He heard the door open, the echoing sound of three pairs of rubber-soled shoes, and the soft breaths of the men, one laboring slightly more than the others as he carried a large jug of water. Alek remained still, eyes closed.

The men drew close to the cage. A buttoned suit cuff made a muffled ting against the bars as Meat reached through to steady Alek's water jug.

Alek remained still, eyes closed.

Water started to move from one jug to the other. Sandy's breathing smoothed out as the jug in his hands grew easier to hold, its weight transferring to the jug being steadied by Meat. The flow of water slowed, the sound changing as the refill emptied. Sandy's feet scuffed against the concrete floor as he started to move back.

Alek struck. The men had forgotten whatever warnings about shifter speed they had been told, lulled by his previous passivity. The shock was evident on their faces as he moved before their prey brains could kick into fight or flight. Alek stomped down on Meat's arm, snapping it against the cross-bars of the cage and trapping him there with body weight. Alek slid his hands through the cage and caught the lapels of a too-slow Sandy, slamming him against the bars. With one hand securing Sandy, Alek withdrew his other, reaching lower to snag Meat's gloriously long ponytail. A sharp twist and the screaming man's neck wrenched enough that he screamed no more.

Big reacted, rushing the bars with the cattle prod. Alek released Meat and caught the prod full into his left hand, his right still a vise grip on the struggling Sandy's jacket and shirt. Pain lanced through him as the electricity in the prod fired and Alek laughed through it as he wrapped his hand around the stick and yanked. Big smashed into the cage bars and rebounded back, the prod now in Alek's hand. Before Big could regain composure, Alek pulled the prod through and flipped it around, his hand on the trigger. He slammed Sandy into the bars twice until the man ceased struggling and sagged, then released him long enough to gain a better grip on his neck, flattening Sandy's body to the bars.

"Tell your boss I would like to talk," Alek said with bared teeth. He doubted that this man had the means to open his cage. It would be better to deal with the head of the snake.

Big stood for a moment in the lights, shaking his head. He wiped blood from where the bars had cut his forehead and stared at his hand, as though if he wished hard enough, all of this would replay differently. It was a testament to his training and character that he calmed his breathing, looked Alek in the eye with a grimace, and nodded before leaving at only a half run.

Sandy woke up and put up another struggle before Alek convinced him with the cattle prod to remain still. They were pressed nearly body to body against the bars, Alek staring down at the frightened man's face and occasionally flexing his grip on the man's neck.

"I'm just following orders," Sandy sputtered, the sad excuse of all men who think working for bad people doing bad things does not reveal their own weakness of character.

Alek bared his teeth again and the man fell silent.

Big did not return. The door opened again and Alek knew from the silence that it was the vampire.

"You were a perfect guest till now," Noah lamented, looking at the mess the quick fight had left. "That man had a family, you know." He gestured to Meat's corpse.

"We all make choices," Alek said. "Does this one have a family? Perhaps we can negotiate now."

"That one? No, he's single with no siblings and his mother died of cancer three years ago. I doubt even she knew who his father was."

"Sir, please," Sandy said, stopping abruptly as Alek squeezed his throat. The man wet himself, the stench mingling with the sharp scent of his fear.

"I would prefer you not slaughter my people," Noah said, his tone still conversational but his silver eyes narrowed.

"I would prefer not to be in a cage," Alek said. "Let me out and no one dies. No one *else* dies," he amended.

"You were so patient, and yet you chose this night of all nights to rebel. Interesting. It is almost like your primal brain knows, perhaps?" Noah cocked his head to the side in a way that reminded Alek of being eyed by an eagle in the forests of his youth. The vampire's words chilled him, raising hairs along his neck and spine.

"Knows what?" he growled.

"Jade has proven troublesome, which I suppose surprises neither of us. She ate Samir's heart, didn't she?"

Alek did not react that he could feel, but perhaps his heartbeat changed for half a breath; perhaps his mouth flattened slightly or his chin rose a touch. Whatever gave it away, whatever confirmed what the vampire suspected, Alek had no control over it, but he saw it in the vampire's face, a certainty, a firmness that had been missing and now appeared between one moment and the next.

"You will be free of that cage soon enough," Noah said, his meaning cryptic, making the words sinister instead of comforting. "I would prefer you not kill anyone else."

Alek looked down into Sandy's hazel eyes. "I learned the hard way that following orders is not always the best idea," he said to the terrified man. He tossed the cattle prod over his shoulder and then used his other hand to help snap the unfortunate minion's neck, releasing the body to slide down the bars.

"Yes, well, enjoy your last night here," Noah said with a grimace that was definitely all for show, though Alek surmised he did it from habit more than desire.

"Jade will come for me," Alek said. "She will never stop coming for me." He knew this in his heart in the way that he knew water was wet and humans died when you separated or crushed the upper vertebra of their necks.

"She already has," Noah said as he retreated into the shadows. "That is the problem. So I am going to have to make you someone else's problem."

Alek shivered, finally feeling the creeping hollowness of fear. He had expected the vampire might kill him if he were no longer useful, though that would incur Jade's wrath forever, but with those parting words, Alek realized death was not to be his fate.

If his instincts were correct, and they were rarely wrong, the vampire was about to hand him over to the First. Death would have been kinder. His fate would likely be far, far worse.

11

Exhausted in spirit and body, we gathered again in the small room where the plan had hatched the night before. This time there was no giddy feeling of reunion, no anticipation. I could barely look in my friends' eyes, not wanting to see pity or grief or perhaps my own roiling tumult of emotions reflected. The drive that had sustained me all through fighting Samir's mind-ghost, dealing with Ainsley, escaping and confronting the vampire, raising Lilith... all of that was drained away, leaving a raw hole in my chest and a heaviness to my limbs.

This feeling had a name. I'd danced with it many times before. When my mother sent me away from the only home and life I'd ever known. After Samir killed Ji-hoon and my second family. When Jasper died. Kneeling in the snow watching Alek dying in front of me while my heart beat in Samir's hand in those moments before I'd turned back time itself and changed the world. Waking and realizing that I'd watched Alek dying in the truck, watching him dying over and over as Samir tortured me through memory and dream.

Despair. I thought it only, not saying the word aloud as people settled in around me. Harper sat close, but not quite touching. The weight of my friends' gazes rested on me like stones crushing the guilty. Expectant gazes, in my imagination, since I lacked the courage to open my eyes. I was supposed to be the big badass. I was supposed to save them.

I curled my legs up onto the cot and squeezed my eyes more tightly shut. The black wave rising in my mind couldn't be allowed to drown me. I choked back the words I wanted to scream at them, these caring, trusting faces that loved me. Didn't they realize I'd always failed everyone? In the end, I had. Every damned time.

"It's late." Ezee's voice pushed through my

hopelessness, gentle and comforting. "The First already has Alek; not much is likely to change in the middle of the night. We can figure out a new plan tomorrow. Freyda said you can sleep in here, Jade. Rosie is bringing blankets."

I wasn't tired, not in a sleepy way. I was just tired down to my core of failing. I wanted Alek back. I wanted his strong arms around me and him telling me it would be okay in his deep voice. I wanted to be able to look him in the eye and tell him the same.

I opened my eyes and met Ezee's dark gaze. "If it were your mate in Schrödinger's proverbial box, would you be able to sleep right now?"

"I'd be doing something rash and likely suicidal," Levi said.

Ezee sighed. "I can't argue with that."

"I'll get snacks, then," Levi said, his forced cheerful tone dragging my attention to him. He stood next to his twin, and while his face held concern, I was relieved that there was no pity there. "All-night planning sessions need snacks."

"I don't have a plan," I said. The words hurt to say aloud, as though they gained more weight, more finality.

"Of course you don't," Harper said sharply. She linked an arm with me and twined her fingers through mine. "You've been in captivity for weeks, we just had a minor wrench thrown into things by that fucking vampire, and we haven't even begun to catch you up on what we know here. If you need time to rest and deal with what happened tonight, it's okay. This crisis has been weeks in the making, maybe months. It can wait a few hours."

Somehow her words did what nothing else had since I'd taken out Ainsley and confirmed that Alek was alive. Tears flooded my eyes and ran down my face before I could so much as blink them away, much less try to stop them. I squeezed her hand and leaned into her strong shoulder, letting myself cry for a few breaths. Letting myself feel and be held.

Levi and Ezee both left, giving us space, and for the first time, Harper and I were alone.

"I failed," I said. "Why do you keep trusting me?"

"Wow, self-pity party at one AM," Harper said.

Her green gaze was intense but kind as I met her eyes. I wiped my tears away with the sleeve of my teeshirt.

"I don't have a plan," I said again.

"What's with the 'I' there, team player? *We* don't have a plan. Yet. And really, we've been waging a sort of guerilla war against the First for weeks. The Alpha of Alphas isn't exactly a pushover or without resources." Harper didn't mention what we both knew from the details they'd given me the night before. They were waging a war, and slowly losing.

She had a point even so. I wasn't alone. This wasn't solely my problem to solve.

"Also, if you think about it, the vampire did us a favor."

"A favor?" I raised my eyebrows, wondering how Captain Optimism here was going to spin this one.

"We already had to deal with the First, right? Well, now we can deal with the First and get Alek back. Two problems, one stone." Harper grinned. "Also, the vampire is gonna to kick himself later when he realizes what a prime opportunity he missed."

I raised my brows higher.

"Have you ever seen a more perfect moment for a 'your princess is in another castle' quote?"

Ezee came back into the room, sparing Harper's life. He was followed by Freyda, Lara, Rose, and Levi. The last three were carrying blankets, bottles of water, and crackers.

"Iollan is recharging in case we need him," Ezee said, glancing between Harper and me. I didn't ask about Brie and Ciaran. They had done what they could, it seemed, and if there was more aid they could render, they would likely have offered. They knew the rules and boundaries of the Fey better than any of us.

"I'm telling Alek you called him a princess," I murmured for Harper's ears only.

"He's going to demand a tiara," she whispered back. Neither of us could quite summon a laugh, but we smiled at each other, much to the confusion of everyone else. Then we got down to business, my heart lighter, friendship lifting the weight of despair so I could get to work.

Levi mentioned that Junebug sent her love but had to sleep—the baby was wiping the floor with her energy levels. We arranged ourselves much as before, and I forced myself to eat a few crackers that tasted like dust while everyone laid out what we knew and didn't know about the First's operations.

What we knew wasn't much. The First had set up a short distance outside Wylde, but seemed to have taken over the RV park as well as a few other key areas around town. There was little way to go in or out of

Wylde without attracting attention, something Freyda and my friends had learned through many losses and hard lessons. There was no solid intel on his numbers, but from what Freyda had gathered from accounts of refugees and her own people, he had at least a couple thousand shifters with him, though an unknown number were there through coercion or mind-control. A lot of them, Freyda guessed, were there because he was the First and whatever he promised worked for them.

While we'd been occupied sleeping or trying to rescue Alek, there had been two small incursion attempts on Brie's shield, but it had been quiet again for the last few hours, as it appeared the First was merely testing this new magic that had arisen. The shield had held.

"Which means he's got eyes on here at all times, probably," I said. Not a comforting thought.

"I know where two of his little spies hide," Freyda said with bared teeth. "I've left them for now. Better to keep them where we know they are."

"No sign of May?" I asked, knowing it was hopeless, but she was the one with the most information about the First.

Freyda shook her head.

"I hate to bring it up, but what about Samir's memories?" Harper asked.

I shook my head. "Those aren't an option at the moment." I didn't know what Samir might know about the First, or if he cared. He'd always been a bit contemptuous of shifters, considering them hardly better than animals. I had never brought up my birth family after one mention because of it. So I didn't even know if he'd realized that the First was both shifter and sorcerer. I don't think he would have believed such a thing was possible.

"I thought you gain the memory of sorcerers you, uh, kill?" Levi said, avoiding saying "eat" at the last moment as he glanced around.

"I do," I said. I'd hoped not to go into this yet, or ever, but they deserved the truth. "But Samir's mind-ghost, the sort of embodiment of his memories, tried to drive me insane and take over my body, so I had Wolf eat him." I realized only a few of the people in the room even knew what Wolf was or that she existed at all.

"Good dog," Ezee murmured with a smile as Lara and Freyda gave me odd looks.

"Why does it not surprise me that even when he's dead Samir is a colossal dick?" Harper gently bumped my shoulder with her own.

"So we don't know where exactly the First is holding Alek," I said, more to myself than to them as I made my mind return to the present crisis.

"If he can't mind-control Alek, I imagine he has to cage him or tie him up and keep him guarded?" Levi looked like he regretted the words even as he spoke them. Ezee elbowed him and glared.

"I think we can trust that Alek is being his usual sweet self," Freyda said with a grim smile.

Her words cheered me. Alek wasn't a helpless, weak kitten stuck up a tree. If he was conscious, he was likely causing all kinds of trouble and working on a way to free himself. Hopefully anything we did wouldn't fuck that up too much.

That thought brought down my mood again. "If we go at the First, he could hurt Alek as retaliation. We don't even know why he wants him, just that May said she thought it was important to the First to keep Alek alive."

"He was supposed to be the heir to the First's power, right? Could he want him for some weird body swap?" Levi caught Ezee's elbow with his hand before his twin could jab his side again.

"Levi, are you actually here to help?" Harper said.

Pushing down the black wave Levi's thought conjured, I shook my head. "Maybe, maybe not. We have to go on the assumption that Alek is alive and that whatever the First wants is still here. Why is he in Wylde at all?"

"Me," Freyda said, her voice a growl. "I'm still the Alpha of Alphas. Many of the stronger pack leaders are here, as well. Whatever the First is planning, we're a part of it somehow. He tried an invitation first, then threats. If he wanted me dead, he would have started with that or overrun us in the last few weeks instead of picking us off one by one. He doesn't like to kill shifters; it seems to be a last resort that even his followers adhere to."

"True," Harper said. "When he mind-controlled the sheriff, he had us surrounded. He could have stormed the place and taken both Vivian and I pretty easily. Instead he spent time trying to use Sheriff Lee to bring us out."

I leaned back against the wall and took a long drink of water from the bottle Rosie had handed me earlier.

So the First wanted shifters alive. Good news, hopefully, for Alek, but also scary in its own way. An enemy that just wanted to kill us was something I was familiar with. Death is absolute, but also simple. Us or him. An enemy who wanted you alive, though? There were too many possibilities for why that was, and most of the ones my exhausted, despairing brain could imagine were too horrible for words.

Especially given that the First was a sorcerer. I knew what we were capable of, and I knew enough to know that there were likely powers and possibilities I didn't yet have a clue about.

The First being a sorcerer also meant that no matter how much everyone wanted to help me, I was going to have to be the one to kill him. He'd invaded my home, killed our people, enslaved others, and was now holding my mate captive. There was only one way this ended for us, no matter what his plans were. Him or me.

In the back of my mind I could almost hear my own voice telling Samir that life wasn't Highlander, but I quelled it. I hadn't pushed things to where they stood now. This was on the First, with events set in motion likely before I even came into the picture, if what little

May had been able to tell us was correct.

"So we just have to come up with a plan to storm the proverbial castle once we figure out where it is, against ten-to-one odds, and then somehow avoid killing anyone we know who is mind-controlled, and save Alek—and Justice May if he's got her. Oh, *and* kill a shifter-sorcerer who is probably older than all of us put together. That about sum it up?" Lara said, the first time she'd spoken during our late-night meeting.

"And I thought I was the little ray of sunshine," Levi muttered.

I went to drink again but found the bottle empty. I crushed it, which kind of hurt my hand, and stood up. "Kobayashi Maru," I said, pacing the short distance between cots.

"But we don't even know the full picture, so we can't say it is impossible," Ezee said.

"What does that mean?" Freyda asked, her brows knitting together. She was not a *Star Trek* fan, apparently.

"It's an impossible test. A no-win scenario," I explained. "If we invade where we think the First is, a lot of people are going to die. We might force him into doing something terrible to Alek, and maybe anyone he's mind-controlled also. May said his powers there weren't infinite."

"Or we'll be fighting in the wrong location and the First will just waltz off," Lara said.

"Or flank us," Levi said.

"And we'll be fighting people from our town, also, family and friends who might have no choice because of his powers," Rose said, her normally cheerful voice grave and hollow.

"Kobayashi Maru," I said again, my brain whirling. Captain Kirk had beaten the scenario by cheating. Fictional character or no, it gave me an idea. Maybe I had been thinking about this the wrong way.

Us or him. Sorcerer pitted against sorcerer.

But I wasn't just a sorcerer any more than the First was. My birth family were shifters. My friends were shifters. The First was also a shifter. If I had broken the world, maybe I could be a shifter, too, though I wasn't going to count on that if I didn't have to. My dragon felt no closer than it had before, even if new and greater power raged beneath my skin.

Shifter justice, shifter ways were not human justice or methods, something Alek had told me time and again. Honor and morality were different, but not missing.

Me vs. him.

"Kobayashi Maru," I said for the third time, a terrible grin slowly spreading across my face as I turned toward the group.

"If you can't win the game," Ezee said.

"Change the rules?" Levi finished.

"Are you thinking what I'm thinking?" Harper asked, her own grin crinkling her eyes as a dawning look of hope, probably mirroring my own, changed her expression in a visible, rising tide as she stood up.

"I think so, furball," I said. "But where are we going to get a gauntlet at this time of night?"

Turned out, the answer was Walmart.

12

There were a lot of protests when my friends learned that I was going to take others to capture the nearby spies in order to deliver my challenge to the First. We'd used Iollan and tree-coastering again to get to the nearest Walmart, where we picked up a list of supplies we could carry, but I could see the strain on the druid. He had done a lot of teleporting around in the last couple days, and there might be more yet to come. I told him to please get some rest, and all but twisted Ezee's arm into going with his husband as well.

Levi grumbled but also went to join Junebug and catch a few hours of sleep. Lara didn't even have to be asked; she saw the writing on the wall and went with a grin and a "good luck." I refrained from telling Harper that was why Lara was employee of the month.

Harper proved to be harder to leave behind.

"What if you need the sword?" she asked.

"We're just going to scare the shit out of a couple shifters, not kill anyone," I said. "Aurelio and Freyda will keep me safe."

"More worried about them than you," Harper muttered.

"If the First accepts the challenge, tomorrow is going to be a long day," I pointed out. "I'll come crawl in with you and let you know the outcome as soon as we're back." She finally relented at that, following her mother away, which showed how tired she actually was, and was being too stubborn to admit.

Freyda and I had developed the plan. Aurelio, who was also known as Softpaw among the wolf shifters, and another pack leader named Tara would come with Freyda, Brie, and me. The Alpha of Alphas was coming because she knew where the spies were, but also for the weight of her title and power. The First likely knew who I was, but it was Freyda he wanted. Same with Aurelio and Tara, for they were both recognizable and powerful alphas of their own packs, and good in a scrap if it came to it. We needed Brie to allow us passage through her ward, and to keep anyone out behind us.

"This is toeing the line of interference," Brie said with a grin that showed she gave no fucks about it as the five of us made our way down the slope from the Den.

"Nah, you're just gatekeeping," I said. Talking didn't matter; we weren't trying to be silent or hide our presence. If Freyda was right, and I had no reason to doubt her, there were two spies hidden well within the old growth of trees at the base of the hill the Den sat upon.

"It will not matter for much longer anyway," Brie said, stretching her arms wide as we approached the slight shimmer of the ward.

"What do you mean?" Freyda asked before I could.

Brie just shook her head and smiled wider.

"See you soon," Aurelio murmured to us before shifting into his wolf.

Tara shifted to her wolf form and followed Aurelio's lead, their bodies disappearing quickly into the deeper shadows beneath the trees. They moved without sound as soon as we crossed the barrier. Brie halted at the edge and folded her arms over her chest. She gave me a little nod when I met her gaze.

Freyda and I continued into the tree line. I was tempted to summon a light, for though false dawn painted the sky more grey than black, under here I couldn't see as well as I wanted. I held my hand up, stopping Freyda, as I remembered I had other options.

Power suffused my blood with warmth as I summoned magic, not to light my way but to change my vision. I'd worked very hard on developing a type of darkvision, but with all the crap happening, it had escaped my mind that I could just solve simple issues like this with magic. I focused and the world brightened, the trees now limned in faint golden light. The world was still black and white, but I could make out leaves and bark, lichen and stone.

Freyda gave me a curious look that made me wonder what my eyes looked like right now, but she shrugged when I motioned we could keep going. We walked, more solidly now that I wasn't afraid of smashing into a tree, moving parallel to where the spies were located. Hairs on my neck rose as I anticipated being watched, but though my vision was very good now, I couldn't make out anything different in the dense forest. Only a few years before I'd hidden in this very tree line, watching the Den and readying an assault to stop a corrupt Justice from murdering all the top wolf-shifters, and now I skulked through it, the weight of our fates once again on my shoulders.

We angled back toward the Den, almost to the edge of the trees. The barrier shimmered about twenty feet from where we walked, visible to my magical sight in a way I wasn't sure others could detect. I'd have to remember to ask the others in the morning.

Freyda stepped close enough I felt the heat of her body against my side and murmured, "Be ready."

It was the only warning I had before Aurelio and Tara burst out of the foliage ahead and to the right of us. They sprang onto what had looked to my vision like stubby tree saplings and brush. Two people, men, from what a glance could tell me, writhed free from what a hunting blind set up on the forest floor. The men shifted to wolves as they tried to slam past us, but I was ready.

Power flew from my hands as I threw my arms wide, stretching magic into a thick barrier around us. I pulled it up into a dome, leaving some room at the top so I didn't accidentally cut off all our air. I wanted a conversation, after all. The wolves hit the barrier hard, the first crumpling with a whine, the second managing to twist his body to take the impact on his side. He crouched next to his companion and snarled at us.

Aurelio and Tara split up to come at the wolves from each side, mindful of where my glowing purple wall cut us off from the rest of the world. The wolves snarled and kept my barrier to their backs, but quickly saw they had nowhere to go as Freyda shifted and cut off the forward path, and the other two alphas hemmed them in from the sides. I'd smashed a few tree branches enclosing us, and had to dodge falling debris while keeping my focus. It was over in a few breaths, just the snarls of the cornered wolves and our own hard breathing breaking up the stillness that settled.

"Great," I said. "Now that we're all friends, let's have a chat." I tied off the spell, knowing it would last only minutes without me pumping magic into it, but I hoped I didn't need more than that.

Freyda shifted back to human. "Do you know who I am?"

The men shifted back to human in a blink, their eyes wide in faces covered with camouflage paint, as though they were straight from a war movie. One was clearly taller than the other, even in their crouched positions. I couldn't tell much more about them, my darkvision flattening colors and shadows to planes and shades of grey.

"The Alpha of Alphas," the taller man said, fear cracking his voice as he got to his feet. He had been the one who managed not to run face-first into my magic wall. The smaller man still crouched, hands down in the dirt, breathing hard.

"Good." Freyda bared her teeth and stepped toward them. Her shoulders seemed broader, her body somehow taking on substance and weight as she squared off, staring down both shifters. They both looked away, not meeting her eyes. "We have a message for the First. One of you is going to die here, and one will live to deliver it. Volunteer for which job you want, but do it quickly."

I looked at Freyda, surprised. We had not discussed anything like that. The plan as talked about had been to run both of the watchers off and let them deliver the message. I knew better than to argue about it now, however. She gave me a very slight smile, and I relaxed a little. Clearly she had a plan behind that threat.

"That's not needed—we'll take your message, both of us," the taller one said.

"Please, Alpha, we're just following orders," the

smaller of the men said, getting to his feet with a wince. Blood ran down from his nose and dripped on his chin, and he wiped it with his sleeve, leaving a swatch of pale skin behind.

"You must deliver the message exactly as we say," I said, and then I pulled the gauntlet from the bag slung across my chest. I hoped Freyda wasn't serious about killing one of them.

They both nodded eagerly, though they gave me a strange look as I stepped forward and extended the gauntlet.

"She will tell you the message," Freyda said, her voice low and sharp. "Your lives depend on this."

"I am Jade Crow," I said. "And I am throwing down the gauntlet. I challenge the First to a duel with me, one on one. Winner take all."

"That's a plastic Infinity Gauntlet," the shorter man said. The taller one elbowed him with a growl.

"You are challenging the First to a duel?" the tall one said as his companion gave him a *what, it is,* sort of look.

"Yes. Eight o'clock tonight, at the old quarry. I will expect the First's answer by high noon," I said, adding the high noon part because it sounded more dramatic.

"Do you have that? Or perhaps your companion will memorize it better with some blood incentive?" Freyda growled.

They both straightened up and the confused looks on their faces faded into fear.

"No, no," the shorter one protested. "I got it. We got it."

"Jade Crow challenges the First to a duel, winner take all. At the quarry," the tall one repeated.

"At eight o'clock," the short one added quickly. "And the First has to accept by noon."

"High noon," the tall one said, glancing nervously at me. He held out his hand for the gauntlet.

I tossed it to him and tried not to chuckle as he carefully tucked it into his shirt as though it weren't an eight-dollar toy from Walmart but a priceless relic of great power.

"When you say, winner take all?" The tall one glanced between Freyda and me again, eyes narrowing. He was definitely the cannier of the two.

"I win, y'all surrender and go away," I said. "If he wins, we'll surrender." I didn't mention that winning meant "one of us kills the other." The First would know what I meant, how this would end. If he didn't know who exactly I was for some reason, he could just ask Alek.

"How does the First get a message back to you?" the short one asked, wiping his face again, though the bleeding had stopped already.

"I'm sure he'll find a way," I said, baring my teeth in what I hoped was an intimidating expression. "It's the twenty-first century. He can use the phone like anyone else. Number for the hunting lodge is online." I dropped the wall with a wave of my hand, the magic giving a little pop as it fell. Somewhere behind me a branch crashed down now that the dome I'd erected wasn't holding it up any longer.

"Go," Freyda commanded them. "Before I change my mind."

They shifted and ran into the trees, heading roughly in the direction of town.

"That went well," Aurelio said as he shifted to human.

"Now we wait," I said softly. Hopefully my challenge had the effect we wanted. Freyda and the others were certain it would. A chance to end all this with a single fight, in a way that appealed to the shifter way of doing things? Not something the First would refuse.

Except he could see the future, if what May had said was correct. I didn't want to think about what that meant if he accepted. Had I already lost? I refused to believe fate was that cut and dried.

"Now *we* rest," Freyda said, placing a firm hand on my shoulder. I didn't miss her emphasis on the "we" part.

I looked again in the direction of town. Somewhere that way, I hoped, was Alek. If things went as planned, I would see him tonight. *Soon, love*, I whispered in my mind. For better or worse, this would end by sunset. Whatever happened, I would need to be ready. With a final glance, I followed Freyda back to where Brie waited as the first blush of dawn stretched sleepy fingers across the sky.

Alek

The vampire left Alek in the cage for long enough that the two dead bodies entered full rigor mortis, the blood and bodily fluids that had leaked from them in death baking under the lights and turning sickly sweet in their smell. Eventually, three men with tranquilizing darts knocked Alek out, though he used the foam pad to try to thwart their efforts. Enough darts hit the mark, and whatever was in them was strong enough, that a heavy darkness folded over him and he could fight no more.

He awoke in chains. A collar was locked tightly around his neck, and his hands were bound behind him, a chain running between the collar and his wrists down his spine. He lay on his side, eyes closed, taking in what his senses could tell him. Someone had put

"Where am I?" Alek asked, not expecting an answer.

"Home," the man said. "Don't you recognize it? No, I suppose not, from here." He looked out the window and then back at Alek.

"Release me," Alek growled as he studied the man. Home. Did that mean Wylde? Or somewhere else?

The man stood about six feet tall, with tanned skin, sandy blond hair, and eyes that were a mix of blue and brown, the irises almost patchwork. His eyes were the most remarkable thing about him. He was not particularly muscular, nor particularly thin, but not fat either. There was a strange looseness to how he stood, and an unfocused feel to his gaze. His scent was a confusing mix of cat and bird, with a faint but sharp hint of sulfur.

"You must live," the man said. "You will understand in time."

"You are the First," Alek said. He did not know what he had expected, but this bland, unfocused man was not quite it.

"Did you think I'd be bigger?" the First said, a smile twitching his pale lips. "People always do." His particolored eyes stared into a middle distance, not quite focusing on Alek.

pants on him, sweatpants by the feel of the m[...] His feet were bare and hobbled together with cuffs and, he assumed, more chain.

The air was different, cleaner, open. Alek picke[d] the scents of other shifters—wolf, mostly, but a m[...] hint of bear and wolverine, too. Beneath those sce[nts] he detected pine sap and lemon cleaning fluid. T[he] floor under his cheek was wood, polished smoot[h]. Light played across his eyelids in a way that spoke o[f] sunlight through tree branches more than artificial light.

Sulfur pricked at his nostrils as he heard footsteps approach and a door open.

"Ah, you are awake." The voice was not one he recognized, smooth and male, neither deep or nor high. Bland, almost toneless, with an accent that could have come from American radio diction classes.

Alek opened his eyes and moved to his knees, unable to rise more with the chains hooked into the floor and the one hobbling his ankles. The room was a cabin with a single door and a single window to Alek's right. Through the window he saw tree branches and light, nothing that told him where he was. He bared his teeth at the man in front of him.

"Why do I have to live?" Alek said. "And if so, why keep me captive here? I have no intention of dying."

"Your life is tied to mine. I have foreseen it. I am only defeated if you die." The First's gaze returned to the room.

"But you tried to kill me in New Orleans," Alek pointed out, hairs on his neck rising as the First looked him over. A buzzing sense of wrongness was growing in the room, a pressure like the weather changing. Pain lanced through Alek's head behind his eyes, but he ignored it and kept his gaze on the First.

"No," the First said. He gave a small shake of his head and the pressure lessened. "That was the others. They learned my weakness. They will not trouble us again."

Sweat trickled down Alek's spine and ribs as his heart rate turned to normal, the headache passing as quickly as it had come. He was reasonably sure the First had just tried to get into his head, but judging from the mildly disappointed look on the man's face, he had failed. Alek hoped.

"When did you have that vision?" Alek asked, wheels turning in his mind.

"You were but a cub. I saw you in the forest. You

took one path and there was death all along it. Then you turned down the other path and it was you who died, and on that path I fell beside you." The First was staring into nothing again, his eyes seeing something no one else saw. "I sent them to bring you, make you a Justice. So I could keep you safe. You are a part of my destiny."

Alek schooled his expression to little more than a snarl, but his shoulders relaxed a hair. If they were in Wylde, it would be only a matter of time before Jade found them. The First was both sorcerer and shifter, something Alek alone could not kill. But his mate could. The First would think he was safe as long as Alek lived, from a vision he'd had half a century before.

It was difficult not to smile. The Fates had not updated the First on his own fate, clearly. For Alek had died already. He remembered, though he was not sure how. He recalled with perfect memory the fight in the Druid's grove. The wound in his chest, the slow beat and stutter of his heart as it struggled, then stopped. Reaching for Jade where she knelt, locked in battle with Samir. His eyes closing despite his desperation and will as the last image he held was Samir ripping Jade's heart from her body.

And then the quiet and the nothing.

Until he was back in the clearing, in the moment before Samir struck them, staring at a whole and healthy Jade.

The First had seen the future, had seen his fate, in a timeline before Jade had changed the world to save them. Alek could not stop the laughter rising in his chest and bubbling forth from his chapped lips.

"Share the joke?" the First said.

"My mate is going to kill you and I am going to watch," Alek said.

"I have seen the future. I know the paths, all the paths," the First said, tone finally entering his voice: a note of anger.

"What is your plan, then?" Alek said, getting the laughter under control. He leaned forward, testing the chains.

"The shifters will bow to me. I will save us all from the fires. Or the sea. It changes. So many things change." The anger was gone as quickly as it had risen, leaving the First sounding vague again.

"Why are you in Wylde? Just for me?" Alek asked, hoping to at least confirm his location.

"The Alpha of Alphas. She is mine. It has been

shown to me. I will show them." The First turned and walked out the door without another word, leaving Alek alone in the cabin.

The chains were fastened to the floor by heavy bolts that groaned but did not budge no matter how he yanked and twisted and pulled. The manacles were forged steel that Alek couldn't get the angle or strength to break. They would have to move him at some point if they did not want him to live in his own filth, so Alek settled into as comfortable a kneeling position as he could find, and waited.

Shadows crawled across the window and stretched cool fingers over the floor of the bare room. Alek tried to comfort himself that he was at least no longer in a vampire's cage, but the encounter with the First had not been reassuring. The First wanted him alive, which was good and bad. Living could be worse than death, depending on how alive and whole the First decided to keep him.

The most disconcerting thing, however, was the First's seeming lack of a plan. Alek had the feeling the First was moving through life at this point guided by visions and memory, things that might happen and things that had not happened at all. There was an edge of madness to the man, just as May had said. Alek did not know how to predict or fight someone whose motives were not just obscured, but perhaps unclear even to the enemy himself.

The First appeared to be going on instinct, too, like an animal. One thing at a time. He was here in Wylde to get Freyda to his side for some reason that Alek was not even sure the First understood. He had Alek now because he believed that Alek had to live or the First would die.

The danger lay not just in the First's powers, though he seemed mercifully unable to mind-control Alek himself, but in his potential randomness. What if his visions updated and showed him that Alek was unnecessary? Or would his visions warn him of whatever moves Jade or Freyda made? Jade had scared the vampire into handing Alek over to the First, which Alek chose to believe was a good sign. His mate was on her feet and trying to get him back.

Alek chose not to dwell on their last moments together, on the blood and the choice she had made at the final second. Whatever those choices changed, he would take it as it came.

The window was dark when the door opened again

and Rachel Lee walked through. Alek perked up, opening his mouth to call a relieved greeting but stopped before more than a word slipped out. Rachel's face was flat, expressionless, her brown eyes empty. She carried a cup of water, from the smell of it, with a bendy straw poking out.

"So he has you?" Alek said softly, sorrow weighing down his chest.

Rachel did not respond. She walked up to him and held out the cup.

"Rachel," Alek tried again to reach her. "You are so strong. I know you can hear me. I will find a way to free you. I promise." He knew it was a promise he might have trouble fulfilling, but he could not just kneel there and say nothing. She was his friend, his companion. They had fought side by side.

She stood silently, no flicker of recognition or response in her expression.

Alek tasted the water. There was no hint of anything out of the ordinary. It tasted like proper well water, clean and clear. His thirst won out and he drained the cup.

As soon as it was empty, Rachel turned around and walked out the door again, turning off the single overhead light, leaving Alek alone again in twilight to watch the branches move in the evening air beyond the window, and wait.

There was no true sleep for him, but Alek found a way to lie on his side that did not cause the collar to strangle him, and he napped in brief, fitful bursts. This prison at least had only natural light, his first taste of darkness in he knew not how long. It was a relief after the unrelenting artificial light in the vampire's prison.

Dawn pushed summer sunlight through his window in a dim glow that brightened with time. His guess was the window faced mostly south, which put the door opening west. Alek noted this as something to catalog, to keep his mind from dwelling on his fears. Once it was light enough to see every detail of his cabin, he spent the early morning testing the bolts and chains. Whoever had made this prison had accounted for shifter strength and size. The bolts were thick and anchored in more than just the flooring. The chains held him at angles where he could not find good leverage or purchase, unable to rise above his knees or reach the walls. Alek realized he was exhausting himself trying to uproot the bolts, and his shoulders were starting to ache from the strain of twisting and pulling with his hands bound behind him, so he ceased his explorations and settled down to wait.

The patient, predatory part of his mind relaxed and watched the door. The mortal, frightened part of him fretted over Jade, over Rachel and whoever else might be caught in the First's magic and control. He breathed in, breathed out, and let the fears go, acknowledging them and then letting them be what they were. There would come a time for action, he promised himself. Until then, he would wait and watch.

The First returned sometime not too long after sunrise, holding a plastic toy glove in his hands.

"Jade Crow has challenged me to a duel," the First said, a bemused tone coloring his otherwise bland voice.

Alek's heart sped up, but he forced himself to remain sitting calmly and not respond.

"I am going to refuse, of course," the First said after a few moments had passed and it was clear Alek was not going to respond. "I have no need for such tactics." He tossed the toy down in front of Alek.

Alek looked at it and recognized the gauntlet from a movie Jade and friends had made him watch. He smiled at her use of symbolism even in this. Not only the gauntlet challenging the First to a duel, but that she had used this one, something that could make and unmake the world, that could change time itself. The gauntlet was a message for Alek, as well.

"You are smart to be afraid of my mate," Alek said, raising his eyes from the gauntlet to the First's face.

"I am not afraid. I have seen the future, the paths. No little sorceress like her can kill me." An edge of annoyance entered the First's voice. "I cannot die while you live."

"If she beats you, the condition is surrender, I am guessing?" Alek asked.

"You mean when I kill her. And yes. Freyda was there to issue the challenge. They said they would surrender if I win." The First paced around Alek, moving like a restless cat in a circuit of the cabin, his gaze a thousand miles away in whatever futures his mind imagined or his powers were showing him.

Alek smiled with bared teeth. "I am sure your control over your people is strong enough that they will not balk to see you afraid and without honor."

The First paced in front of Alek again and lashed out, gripping Alek's chin with a strength Alek had not predicted. He felt the bone of his jaw grind from the pressure of the First's fingers.

"I am not afraid. She is not a shifter. Her challenge is meaningless. I made you. I gave you power beyond what you would ever have been if I had left you in Siberia."

"Then take it back," Alek said, leaning away, trying to free his aching jaw.

"Your mate is nothing," the First said, his face in Alek's face, eye to eye, his breath warm and sulfurous.

"She was born to shifters," Alek said through gritted teeth. "And you cannot take my powers back, can you? That scares you, too. I smell it." He reeled back and barely kept himself on his knees as the First released his grip.

"Do you think to distract me?" the First said. "Does Jade plot to free you? Would she kill you if she knew it was the only way to defeat me? She led you down the path of death and into shadows that even I could not pierce but you are home now. Where you belong."

"I belong to Jade, forever," Alek said. "She is my home. Her heart is my heart, her path my path. If my death will keep her safe from you, I will find a way to die." He followed his instincts, striking where he sensed weakness. Whatever Jade's plan was, she wanted to fight the First one on one. Alek would give her whatever aid he could, even if it was just goading the First into doing what Jade desired. He would trust she had a plan.

"No," the First said, his voice little more than a growl. For once, his gaze was focused on Alek, clear and dangerous. He bent and snatched up the gauntlet. "I am not afraid, but you will be. You will watch tonight as I kill your mate. You will see that my path is the only path. The future is written, Aleksei. I will prove it to you, to all of you, in blood."

With those chilling words, the First stalked from the cabin, slamming the door behind him.

Alek worked his sore jaw back and forth, testing it. He resumed his seated position and shook out his shoulders as best he could, flexing tingling fingers. Tonight, the First had said. Then Alek would wait. Tonight he would see Jade, finally. He had done what he could.

13

"One of the spies we rousted last night was at the bottom of the hill, waving a white flag," Freyda said. "Well, a pillow case, anyway."

We were arrayed around a table in the great hall, eating a late breakfast, though from my companion's faces, I guessed nobody had slept a whole lot more than I had. Faces at other tables turned, watching the Alpha of Alphas where she stood at the head of the table, speaking to me but also pitching her voice so that everyone in the hall could likely hear her. Silence flowed like a wave over the huge space until we all waited to see what the messenger had said.

Freyda waited another moment, her gaze fixed on

me. She gave a slight nod.

"The First has accepted Jade's challenge. Eight o'clock tonight, at the quarry."

I couldn't read her well enough to know how she felt about it. I knew I was taking a huge risk, but it was the only way out I could see that wouldn't lead to more bloodshed and potentially having to fight and kill our friends and neighbors. I was fully aware that, win or lose, it would probably be Freyda shouldering the bulk of the work to settle and reunify and punish those who survived. She would be the one picking up the pieces.

Talk resumed, subdued, but the air had changed from grim determination to excitement, the hall buzzing as speculation spread. My job would begin and mostly end tonight. First, I had to win. Then I could worry about how to help salvage my hometown and the shifter population here.

"Think he'll have Alek with him?" Harper asked.

"I don't know," I said, my mind whirling. I had mere hours to ready myself for a sorcerer duel. I needed quiet.

"We're going with you," Ezee said, his tone firm. I made a face but wasn't going to argue. I'd already assumed nobody was going to let me walk into the duel alone.

"You challenged the First—that means he gets to pick the weapon, right?" Levi said.

"He's a sorcerer, I'm a sorcerer," I said, whole new worries gnawing a hole in my belly at Levi's words.

"He's also a shifter," Junebug said. "He's unlikely to choose pistols, at least."

I almost protested that I wasn't *that* bad a shot, but Junebug was a crack shot and I was amateur hour with a gun despite lots of training with my friends. I didn't like guns at all, and I felt like the guns could tell.

"I'm going for a walk. Alone," I said. "I need to prepare."

"We all need to prepare," Freyda said. "How many should go with you, do you think?"

"Will the First stick to the rules?" I asked. We were a little fucked if he didn't.

Freyda chewed her lip and then nodded. "Yes. Honor is important. Word of this will spread, and he cannot control all his people with magic. If he breaks the rules of the duel, he will look fearful, weak. That could give us an opening if we need it."

"Good," I said. "I'm not intending to lose, but we need contingency plans. How to protect people who can't fight, or shouldn't fight," I added, glancing at

Junebug. She made a face but put a protective hand over her belly. "What to do if I lose." Those last words were hard to say, but we had to face all realities.

Freyda glanced meaningfully around the great hall before she said, "The terms are our surrender." Her eyes told me she knew I never meant for them to stick to the terms if I lost. Surrender was not actually an option.

There was honor, and then there was survival. The two didn't always play nicely together. Freyda had no intention of broadcasting that, which was fair. There were a couple hundred shifters here, many we didn't know well. If word got to the First that we had no intention of honoring the terms, he might not stand up to fight me.

The duel was my best shot at killing him without anyone else getting hurt. What happened after that, well, I'd torch that bridge when we crossed it.

The day was warm, bordering on hot, the sun high in the sky and wildflowers scattered over the open field around the Den. I made my way almost to the barrier, trusting Brie's magic to protect me, but wanting to put as much space between myself and anyone else as I could.

I sank into the grass, letting the sun warm my face and the soft summer breeze surround me with the buzz of insects and scent of growing, living things. Life went on around me, oblivious to the turmoil inside me and the dangers of the world. Tonight, I would end this and get Alek back. After that… I stopped the thought. Whatever I had done to the world by killing Samir, it was done now. No use borrowing trouble, as Rosie would say.

I let my magic flow through me, reveling in the strength of it. Despite too little sleep and all the trials I'd been through in the last few weeks, my magic wasn't suffering. Power sang in my blood in a way I'd not felt maybe ever, ready, waiting, seemingly endless, though I wasn't going to count on that part being actually true. I knew burnout intimately.

Closing my eyes, I visualized my dragon. I reached for the fire at my core and called to her, inviting wings to unfurl and claws to unsheathe.

Nothing physical happened, though I felt my dragon move inside me like a physical weight pressing against my bones. The ability to shift that I'd had beyond the Veil was not a power I had carried to the real world. I let the fire go and opened my eyes.

If the First did not choose magic, I would make do. If I was losing, I would cheat. Kobayashi Maru. Survival is better than honor.

Alek would understand, I knew. He would tell me that the scales would balance in the end. Fight, and live.

If I broke the rules, the duel would end and the battle would begin. People would die. I took a deep, shuddering breath. I would save who I could, drain myself to the last drop of power if I had to.

"He'll choose magic," I said aloud. "He's a sorcerer." The First clearly wasn't afraid to use magic, with his mind-control and what he'd done to Justice May's wounds. I had no idea how powerful he was, though I was going to place my money on "very" if I had to. Underestimating an unknown enemy seemed unwise.

But I was stronger than I had maybe ever been. I'd defeated Samir, though I'd used a magic blade to help with that. I had taken on every challenge thrown at me and survived.

Not everyone survived, the voice of my deepest fears whispered to me. I told that voice to fuck off. I was alive, and so I could find a way to not repeat my past mistakes.

This time, I would win. I had to. Whatever it took.

I got to my feet, letting my magic slide back into the deep pool inside me. First, however, I had to go see a druid about a ride.

"Why is there a unicorn here?" Harper asked as those of us who were going to head to the quarry assembled in front of the Den.

"That's my ride," I said, grinning at Iollan where he stood at Lir's head, one hand resting against the unicorn's neck.

"I don't remember this part of the plan," Ezee said.

"It's not," I said. "I just want to arrive looking like a badass."

Iollan had agreed to ask if Lir would do this for me, though the unicorn owed me his life, so I didn't see him saying no. The Druid had told me that he'd be asking his own favor from the unicorns, and warning me that Lir would have orders to get Ezee and Levi out if things went sideways. I had a feeling that Iollan hadn't told the twins this part, but I had zero objections.

I also wanted to conserve my physical strength. We were going on foot to the quarry, the shifters coming with me in their animal forms, and I didn't fancy wasting magic or walking that whole distance.

Iollan boosted me onto Lir's back. I scooted so that I was balanced, riding up almost on his withers. I twined my fingers into the unicorn's silvery hair. I had forgotten how damn soft they were.

"Thanks," I whispered, leaning over Lir's neck. He tossed his head as I sat back up and looked around.

"I feel like I should make a Crispin's Day speech or something," I said to the admittedly motley company of thirty or so shifters. Ezee, Levi, Harper, and Lara stood closest to me, flanked by Aurelio and two women I recognized as being from his pack.

"We can probably skip the speeches," Freyda said. "Everything is in place here." She nodded to the alpha, Tara, who had come with Aurelio and us in our dawn assault on the spies. Tara nodded back, her expression grimly determined.

I took a deep breath and gently squeezed my legs, signaling Lir to start forward. The unicorn knew where we were going; my job was to not fall off before we got there.

"Times up," I couldn't resist saying. "Let's do this."

Whoops and cheers followed me, then faded away as the people around me flowed into wolf and fox, bear and badger, coyote and cougar. Together we marched down from the Den, past Brie as she held the barrier open for us, and out into the summer twilight.

14

The best part about riding a unicorn was that I was riding a freaking unicorn. The worst part was that it took us nearly an hour at a steady pace to go from the Den to the quarry. All my friends were in animal shapes, a small sea of fur around me as we went overland, avoiding roads and taking a path Freyda had already sent scouts out along for our safety. It appeared the First wasn't setting traps, though Freyda's scouts had reported he'd set up at the old quarry a few hours before we left. We didn't have the numbers to get there first and contest anything, so we'd be the later arrival.

The advantage was that it was home turf. I'd fought a battle with an assassin there before and was somewhat familiar with the layout of the place. It was close to town but far enough out that we could sling spells or wage a battle without bringing in human authorities or harming anyone not present. There wasn't much there to burn and the ground was pretty open, especially in the main gravel pit where we were headed.

The absolute worst part of the ride was the time it gave me to think about what was happening. I hoped I'd see Alek, but I also worried he'd be mind-controlled or worse. My brain was happy to offer up what the "worse" could look like, to the point that Lir snorted and gave his body a shake, bringing me out of my thoughts and reminding me where I was. I dug my fingers deeper into his mane and whispered, "Thanks."

It was hard to not second-guess the plan. Hard not to immerse myself in worry the fight wouldn't go in my favor. With all the fights I'd had before, they either happened so quickly that I didn't have time to do more than react, or there had been so much to do leading up to them—more fighting usually— that I hadn't the time to get into my own head.

If I lost, the First wouldn't just kill me. He would gain access to my power, all my powers. All Samir's powers, and Tess's, and every sorcerer and magic user

I'd consumed. But beyond that, he'd gain my memories. Every private and intimate or terrible or happy moment, every loss. Every triumph.

I wouldn't just lose my life, I would be handing it over in its entirety to another.

The weight of that hit me as we came in sight of the quarry. The weight of all I had done, all I'd become, and how quickly what I was could vanish, could be stolen by another. I thought of Tess, especially, in that moment. How she sacrificed everything to give me her power and her memories, hoping I would defeat Samir.

Her sacrifice had not been in vain. I'd defeated Samir. I was determined I would defeat the First. Losing meant losing too much that I was not willing to give.

We slowed as we filed into the main pit. Shifters lined the sides of a makeshift arena that had been erected there, most of them in animal form as they perched on boulders and rocks and piles of dirt around a large, shimmering circle etched into the open center.

Sulfur teased my nose, souring the summer breeze, alerting me to the First's presence even though I was unsure which of the humans who waited in front of us was him. The shifters with me spread out in a wedge with me as their point, and we proceeded into the center, approaching the glowing circle.

Alek! My heart sang as I spied my mate, though he knelt in chains held by two women, I caught his fierce gaze. It was all I could do not to summon power and turn those chains to dust around him. Until that moment I'd known he was alive, but in the way that I know platypuses are real. I believed because I wanted it to be true and I'd been told it was true. Seeing him, even kneeling in chains with his hair loose and unwashed, his ribs standing stark in his skin, his eyes burning with life, it was my everything. I felt like my heart had finally started beating again.

"You are early," a man said, drawing my eye away from Alek. He stepped forward, a white man with a tan that spoke of many hours in the outdoors. He was a few inches taller than I, putting him near six feet. He was of average build, almost everything about him invoking the word *non-descript*, except his eyes. His irises were a mix of brown and blue like continents and oceans on a map.

Lir knelt to let me step down with my dignity intact. The unicorn tossed his head again and then leapt to the side, clearing a good thirty feet of ground as he shone silver for a moment and then disappeared. I knew he wouldn't go far, if Iollan had made a deal with him. This left me standing about ten feet away from the First, flanked by Freyda and Harper as they came up beside me.

The women beside Alek, the ones holding the chains attached to the chains at his waist and his collar, lifted their faces, staring at me with blank eyes. Rachel and Vivian. That fucking bastard. They were clearly still under his control; no recognition or even sign of thought flickered in their expressions.

"You must be the First asshole," I said to the bland-faced man. I could smell the sulfur of his magic even from here and see the way the red glow of the circle almost bent toward him.

"Freyda," the First said, ignoring me. "Will you adhere to the terms?"

Freyda growled. "Will you?"

"You will trust me in time," the First said, giving a vague wave of his hand.

"Alek," I said, stepping toward my mate.

"No," the First snarled. "He is not yours. You will die here and he will be free of you."

"I love you," Alek said but I knew from his slight smile and the look in his eye that while he meant those words, what he really wanted to say was: "Do you have a plan?"

"What is that circle?" I said, deciding that the First's words weren't worth answering. He was clearly not entirely okay in the head.

"We will fight in there. Nothing can cross without my permission."

That threw a wrench in the "Harper will throw me the Alpha and Omega or charge in with it if shit gets dicey" backup plan.

"I don't like it," I said. "That wasn't in the terms."

"You and me. No one else. No interference. Those are the terms," the First said, bland equilibrium back in his voice. "I am told you were born to shifters. We will fight as our people fight, with honor. No sorcery, no weapons. Tooth and claw alone."

Well, shit. I had human teeth and no claws to speak of. My nails had grown a bit in captivity, but I'd clipped them in the shower, and even if I hadn't, they were hardly claws.

"Jade is not a shifter," Freyda said. "I will stand in as her champion if these are your terms."

"No," I said quickly as a small smile broke the flat affect of the First's face. "This is my duel. My challenge. I will fight."

I might've had a slim chance, but I knew in my bones that Freyda had none at all, no matter how strong she was. The First had three shapes: eagle, snake of some sort, and tiger. Tiger versus wolf alone was probably game over, and the First was more than just a shifter. Freyda couldn't kill him.

We stood a chance with me, at least. Either I'd find a way to cheat, or I would find a way to summon my dragon, thus staying technically inside the rules. Perhaps earlier, in the field, she just hadn't had the proper incentive. We were too late now for second thoughts or regrets. This was my fight, and I was taking it.

"I could fight as her champion," Alek said. He had a strange smile, as though he knew the First would refuse.

The First shook his head. "No champions. We fight to the death, winner take all."

He raised his voice for that last part, the words carrying to the gathered shifters. By my count there were at least two hundred in the bowl of the quarry alone, and I had a feeling the rest weren't far away. Freyda's scouts had said there'd been a lot of movement and vehicles that way. If it came down to desperate times, I knew which directions to start flinging the fireballs.

Except Alek, Vivian, Rachel, and who knew who else among the missing Wylde shifters were also in that direction. Things would get messy and maybe tragic. Exactly what we were trying to avoid.

Freyda would free Alek if I fell. She'd promised me this. The small force we'd brought with us was distraction; the bulk of our side would be using this duel to infiltrate from the flank, subduing hopefully smaller groups as they went and crippling vehicles and means of communication. My job was to kill the First but if I failed, it was to keep everyone there occupied as long as I could. And, if it truly came to it, to use magic and turn the tide in our favor. That was the last resort, because it would mean so much death.

"Jade?" Harper murmured. Her green eyes were concerned as I turned to her. She lightly touched the hilt of the sword.

I gave her a small shake of my head and turned back to the First.

"Fine. We fight in your circle. Tooth and claw. No sorcery."

"Jade," Alek murmured, my name a prayer on his lips. His ice-blue eyes held total trust and love. An ocean of it. For a moment I again contemplated blasting him free and taking us out of here.

But that would only solve one problem, short term. It was time to adult up and fight.

"After you," I said to the First, motioning to the arena.

15

He stepped into the arena, passing through the red glow as though it were mist. I followed, magic singing in my veins as I prepared for treachery or an attack.

His magic circle felt cool against my skin, causing gooseflesh to rise on my arms as I walked through. That was the only effect. Sound passed through just fine, and I heard as much as saw from the corner of my eye as Freyda and my friends moved forward to line one side. Alek's chains clinked as Vivian and Rachel allowed him to pivot so he could face the arena and watch. I laid a hand against the red glow. It felt the way the Noah's ward had, solid and unyielding.

One way street at that point. The First had let me

in, but wasn't going to let me out again. Not alive, anyway.

Too late now. I turned and walked further into the area. The sun had mostly set, leaving a bright summer twilight. The heat of the day had passed. We'd chosen this time to make sure nobody would have the sun in their face and so that our secondary forces could work with more shadows on their side.

"So what's your name and why is it Bob?" I asked as we faced off, the First pacing across the circle away from me. The arena was about forty feet in diameter, enough distance we could get away from each other, but not enough to go far.

"I am the First," he said. He had walked about twenty feet from me before turning. Behind him, outside the circle, more shifters closed in, though none came within a foot of the barrier.

"You'll be the Last," I said, not one to leave low-hanging fruit untouched.

The First laughed with a harsh bark. "I have seen our futures, Jade Crow. You are not in them."

That was not a comforting thought. But I knew from my own brush with time manipulation and the Pattern that the future wasn't set in stone. It was malleable, changeable, every choice branching into new futures.

I spread my hands and thought again of my dragon. I visualized her from the tufts of my ears to the tips of my black wings and long tail. Fire burned in my belly, warming me from the inside, but my dragon form did not manifest. It felt like my skin was too tight, as though stretched to contain the dragon but not yielding to let her out.

The First shifted into a giant golden eagle and shot upward with heavy beats of his wings. Grit flew into my face and I ducked instinctively. He flew high and circled.

"Oh, so you get to leave the arena?" I muttered. I bent and found two good-sized rocks, hefting one in each hand.

The First dove for me, as I'd guessed he would. I hurled the rocks at his incoming shadow, both missing terribly. Throwing had never been my thing, but I scooped up more gravel and cast it at his wings as they spread to arrest his dive.

His claws raked my arms, tearing into me as I dropped to protect myself. White-hot pain seared down my forearms. I threw my body weight into the eagle, bringing us both to the ground. I'd seen videos of fish drowning eagles and wished in that moment I had a lake. But all I had was rock.

Still, rocks and feathers seemed like they'd be a terrible combination. Using my body weight and trying to breathe through the pain, I rolled onto the eagle. Grounded, his wings beat against the gravel, kicking up dust and grit. Then the First shifted again, becoming some kind of huge snake, a python perhaps, his scales sharp and cool beneath me. He writhed, his thick, muscular body tossing me like a twig away from him. I rolled, trying to remember all of Alek's lessons in hand-to-hand combat, and made it back to my feet.

The First slithered away and reared up. Not a python. He was a cobra, the wide hood spreading as he hissed at me, forked tongue flicking out. The dust we'd kicked up swirled in the breeze and coated my bleeding arms. A weak cheer went up from the First's side of the arena, not nearly as many voices as I would have expected for the numbers he had. I hoped that was a good sign for us.

"Jade?" Harper's voice cut through the cheering. I heard someone, a man, say something to her. One of the twins, probably. I didn't spare a glance behind me, my gaze locked on the cobra.

My magic whispered in my veins and begged my hurt body to use it. *Not yet*, I told it. The First was toying with me, but it was buying Freyda's people time. Everyone was watching us. I wasn't losing too badly, yet. A little blood and pain was nothing. The deep gouges in my arms didn't feel like nothing but mind over body and all that.

Breathing deep through my nose, I circled toward where I knew Alek watched, wanting him at my back, wanting the reassurance he was there.

"Shift, Jade," Alek murmured as the First circled with me, slithering closer. Gravel crunched beneath my feet and blood slid down my arms, spattering the rocks.

"I can't," I whispered, knowing he would hear me. "I tried. It isn't working." I wished more than anything to turn and look at Alek's face but I didn't dare give the First my back.

The First didn't like us talking. He struck faster than I could track, his fangs slicing into my left shoulder as his muscular, scaled body wound around me. I was yanked off my feet, my arms locked to my sides with crushing force as the First dragged me into the center of the arena. Ice flowed from my shoulder wound as the First let go with his fangs. Venom. I hoped I was immune though from the intense, paralyzing cold spreading down my left side, I was guessing I wasn't. My sorceress healing would keep me from dying, but it wasn't a miracle working at the speed of injury.

The snake's coils pulled tighter. I felt my ribs crack. The air in my lungs wheezed out of me and I couldn't stop a pained cry from escaping my lips. The First coiled tighter and tighter as I struggled. Red dots danced in my vision and darkness and pain narrowed my world to the fight to take just one more breath.

Play time was over.

I reached for the ocean of power inside me. I'd known I couldn't win without either figuring out how to shift into a dragon or without cheating and using magic. I hoped I'd bought enough time for Freyda's people to help. I hoped I wasn't dooming everyone I loved to die in battle. I hoped I still had enough strength in me to finish this one way or another.

A roar split through the rushing of blood in my ears. A deep, coughing tiger roar. The coils around me loosened and then dropped me. I crawled away from the First, toward that beautiful, familiar roar. *Alek.* The sound vibrated into me, my skin tight and growing tighter. I sucked in a painful but beautiful breath of fresh air.

Alek's roar sounded again, more forceful this time. A shadow fell across where I lay gasping on the sun-warmed rocks as the First shifted into a huge tiger and stalked over me, his mouth full of teeth as long as my forearm. He also roared, but his was weaker than Alek's. My mate's voice was inside me now, deep in my bones, in the rush of my blood, the beat of my heart.

My skin was too tight. Heat bloomed inside me, pushing back the paralyzing cold in my shoulder, burning away the pain of the wounds in my arms. My arms. Scales. I saw them beneath my skin, deep purple and silver.

Alek's roar, his power, was calling my dragon.

I reached for her again, and it felt like a membrane broke inside me in a burst of heat. The pain of my broken ribs, torn arms, and damaged shoulder went from doomful to merely aching. My vision sharpened, my breathing evening out as I gained my feet. Paws. My paws!

The First sprang back and shifted again, this time

into his human form. "No," he yelled, his face twisting with rage.

I knew what he saw, what they all saw as his people, all shifted into their animal forms by Alek's power, moved away from the arena circle in a frightened wave of fur and shifting bodies.

Head like a cat's, but with scales. Ears tufted with soft black fur. Big black wings with deep purple scales, and a long, scaly tail that ended in its own tuft of fur. A compact, strong body with purple and silver-tipped scales shimmering along its length. I dwarfed the First as I reared up on my hind legs and spread my wings, flexing the claws in my front paws. He wanted tooth and claw, well, he was welcome to come get some.

"This is sorcery," the First sputtered. "You are cheating. You do not win here. I saw it. I cannot be defeated while he lives." The sharp smell of sulfur grew stronger and red sparks flickered and fell from his clenched fists as he advanced on me.

Before, with everyone I'd ever fought, even Samir, I'd hesitated at the last. Debated the kill, even when there hadn't really been time to do so. This time, Dragon-me was out of fucks to give.

"I cannot be defeated!" the First yelled again, his

bland face twisted into a mask of rage. Spit flecked his lips. Gravel vibrated into the air as his magic grew and swirled around us in sulfurous red smoke. "I cannot…"

Reader, I ate him.

16

Silence followed. The circle snapped as I crunched and swallowed. I did my best not to think about what I'd just done, or there was a good chance the First would be coming back up. A vomiting dragon-cat might be on brand, but it would hurt my currently badass image. Wolf appeared in my mind's eye, corralling the First's memories before I could more than glimpse them. I sent her a mental thanks. I was up for one crisis at a time at this point. His magic sank into the ocean of my own.

I spread my wings and used magic to raise me into the air, not wanting to kick up a dust storm by beating my wings. I had no idea if I could speak in this form, but I was going to try. Below me stretched a few hundred bodies, still mostly in their animal forms, but some had shifted back to human. The walls and ridges of the quarry were swarmed and all their eyes turned upward to me as I hovered overhead.

"The First is dead," I said. My voice rang forth, almost musical, a deep toll of a bell across open land. It wasn't so much from me moving my mouth, either—I felt my words as a projection more than an actual act of speaking. More magic I supposed, but I ran with it. There'd be time to figure out this whole dragon thing later.

"Surrender, and you can go back to your lives. This is my town. If you were coerced to be here, you will have our help. If you chose the wrong side, you have until dawn to be far far away." I punctuated the last words with a strong wingbeat and a roar of my own that reverberated around the quarry and shook the branches of the distant trees.

I lowered my body back to the ground. Even in this form, my ribs ached and my mouth tasted like sulfur and blood. I released my dragon form, visualizing fingers and hair, focusing on the feel of my D20 amulet against my chest. Pain returned with a vengeance as I shifted back to human shape. I shoved it aside and turned away from the confused and frightened bodies of the First's people.

I stumbled toward where Rachel and Vivian were trying to help Alek out of his chains. Harper, Ezee, and Levi moved toward me but stopped as I waved them off. Freyda went past me, toward the hopefully former enemy, Aurelio and others following her lead. They parted for me as I got to Alek. His chains turned to dust with a tired wave of my hand, my magic flowing strongly through my veins, holding the darkness at bay.

And then I was in his arms, his warm skin against my cheek, his heartbeat strong as I laid my ear to his chest. I used more magic to push away the world, surrounding us in a swirling circle of cooling mist. Time slowed for us, the chaos beyond blocked out. Whatever happened next, this was worth it. This moment was all I'd fought for.

"I remember my first vision of you," Alek murmured, his voice rumbling in his chest.

"When you came into my shop and accused me of murder?" I said with a hiccupping laugh. My face was wet with tears, and I didn't even remember crying. It hurt to cling to him and I didn't care at all. The pain made me wrap my arms more tightly around him.

"Before that. The vision from the Council that sent me to you. A woman with hair like smoke and flames in her eyes."

I tipped my head back and looked up at him. "I remember. I stood all poetically at the crossroads between life and death." I licked my lips as he bent down, his mouth a breath away from mine. Beyond my magic, the real world was trying to invade, the sounds of shouting and flickers of movement breaking through the mist. "I wonder which I chose?"

Alek's lips brushed mine and then he tucked me against his chest again, resting his chin lightly on my head. "Love," he murmured. "You chose love."

Freyda, Aurelio, and the other wolf-shifter alphas took control of things after that. I don't know how they got it all sorted, and I knew there were some scuffles, but no one died. There were a lot of shifters displaced who would need help finding new homes or returning to their old lives, but Freyda was like a general with a plan and I was smart enough to stand aside and let her do what she was good at.

I went home, taking Alek with me. After food and a shower and about a million years of sleep, but really only fifteen hours or so later, I felt like a person again. My shoulder and ribs healed in what felt like record time while I slept. A corner had been turned with my shifting into a dragon. I understood somewhat better what the Archivist had meant when he said he felt change coming. I had eaten Samir's heart and broken a seal. Change was inevitable.

Fortunately, so were pancakes and bacon. The world wasn't totally wrecked yet.

17

"You really going to eat that sitting on his lap?" Lara asked me as I set my heaping plate down in front of Alek before squishing into his lap.

"I'm not letting him go ever again, so get used to it," I said with a grin.

"You need to eat, and I need to eat." Alek wrapped his arms around me and gently lifted me up, setting me in my own chair. He kept his thigh pressed against mine, however, and his eyes were crinkled with laughter as I made a face at him.

I knew I couldn't stay in actual physical contact with him forever, but I wasn't about to relinquish it when I didn't have to yet. Part of me couldn't believe he was real. It was going to take more than a day or two for me to forget the sight of his face covered in blood, the sound of him dying beside me as I hung helplessly trapped in the truck. I was resilient, not impervious. There were still haunted shadows deep in his eyes, too, and for all he joked about it, he hadn't stopped touching me, either.

Harper, the twins, and Junebug had shown up with Lara this afternoon, all of them toting various baked goods and supplies. We crowded around my table eating a late breakfast and enjoying the feeling of nobody trying to kill us. They caught me up on what Freyda and the others were doing. Vivian and Rachel were apparently in the thick of things at the Den still, doing what they could to help. Harper looked happier and less burdened, so I assumed when she shared the news about the vet and the sheriff, it meant she'd gotten a chance to talk to them. There was no way they would blame her for running, and I hoped that with their help she would stop blaming herself.

Justice May also returned, having been in hiding with a couple of shifter families. She'd been pinned down by a group of the First's minions, but they'd been called away before the big duel and she was able to escape with the refugees. She was going to be staying on with Freyda for a while and helping with the rehoming of various groups.

I decided to keep the shop closed for a couple more days. I took the time to rest, eat, and spend a lot of time in bed with Alek. Three days after the fight with the First, I came upon my warded box as I was cleaning the apartment. I opened it and laid my hand over Samir's key.

Wolf materialized and brushed against my side, pushing her nose under my opposite hand. I dug my fingers into her fur as a wave of memory, Samir's memory, rocked me. Like a proper wave, it flowed through me and then was gone again, leaving knowledge in its wake.

"Jade?" Alek said, coming up beside me, his ice-blue eyes concerned.

"I know what it is," I said. Awe shivered through me. "I know what this does!"

Alek helped me hang the door that Samir had sent me onto a closet in the storeroom. It fit perfectly, morphing slightly to fill the space it needed as we screwed in the hinges. I tried not to think about the magic that had created this door. Samir was dead. I knew the door's purpose now, and it wouldn't hurt me.

I tested the key anyway before I sent text messages around and gathered the gang. Just in case, like a good rogue checking for traps.

I ushered Harper, Lara, Ezee, and Levi into the storeroom. Alek leaned against the doorway behind them as they all filed in and stared at the ornate door on the closet.

"I thought that door was evil?" Lara asked, brows raised.

"Nope," I said. "I know what it does now." I motioned to the key in it. "Who wants to do the honors?"

No one stepped up. In fact, they backed away.

"Oh come on," I said. "It's fine. I checked it for traps and everything."

They all had more or less flattened themselves to the far wall.

"For fuck's sake, that was *one* time. One! In a game, not even real." I made a face at my friends.

"Total," Harper said.

"Party," Ezee said.

"Kill," Levi said.

"What about you?" I said to Lara. "Come on, be brave!"

"Oh no," Lara said, folding her arms over her chest. "I'm a gay black woman, and I have seen this movie."

"Fine, cowards," I muttered, ignoring Alek's soft chuckle. I turned the key and swung the door open.

The gasps behind me were satisfying at least. The door opened into a library, a proper huge library with shelves stacked to the heavens and long wooden ladders on brass wheels at various intervals.

"Is that…?" Ezee moved forward and peered over my shoulder through the doorway.

"Samir's library? Yeah," I said. "Only, don't go touch anything, sorry. I haven't actually checked the whole house in there yet."

"His house?" Harper said. "Maybe we should burn it. To be safe."

I couldn't say the thought hadn't occurred to me, but I believed that the value of the works he had collected outweighed the risks. There were very probably things in that house I was doing to destroy with impunity, but it would take a while and careful sorting, and careful access to his memories, to sort it all out.

"Some stuff I will destroy, for sure," I said. "Once I figure out what it all is and what it does."

"I'll totally help you sort the books," Ezee said as an excited gleam lit his eyes.

"I figured you would," I said, sliding an arm around him. "Anyway, I figured y'all should be the first to see this. After everything."

"After everything," Harper said, coming up beside me. "We're still here."

"Yes we are, furball." I slid my other arm around her and we stared through the magic doorway into our future. It looked pretty bright indeed.

18

That evening I stood in the lot behind my building, watching the sun sink into the trees. Alek and I had taken our dinner down to the picnic table on the back patio, enjoying the warm summer breeze. He stood behind me, his arms loosely wrapped around my torso, his chin resting on my head.

The wind carried the scent of baking bread and crushed lavender. We both tensed as three figures appeared in front of us as though by magic, stepping out of beams of sunlight as though through doorways we just hadn't noticed. Alek stepped away from me, moving to my side, his muscles tensing.

The three women all looked somewhat like Brie, but

not. The tallest had sharper features, her blood-red hair smooth instead of curly, her eyes black with flecks of silver in the irises instead of bright blue. She stood in the middle. The woman to her left was the shortest; her features reminded me of a bird's, inquisitive and alive, her hands seemingly unable to keep still as she smoothed her green dress. Her hair was more orange than red, the curls loose and unruly, and when she met my gaze, flames danced in the pupils of her light blue eyes.

It was the third woman who looked most like Brie, her rounded face cheerful and sweet, her bright blue eyes almost the same, though gold lines like sunbeams darkened the irises. She wore an apron and jeans, and her red curls were piled on her head in a messy bun held by a single, straining green ribbon.

"Airmid?" I guessed, looking at her. "And you're Brigit," I said, motioning to the fire-eyed woman. "And that makes you Macha." I glanced at the tall woman, trying to contain my nerves. I'd known for years who, and what, Brie was, but being faced by three goddesses was different than knowing they existed.

"Relax, Jade," Airmid said. "And you can keep calling me Brie. I've gotten used to it and I'll be sticking around."

"You all won't be?" I asked, not sure if I felt sad or relieved.

"I have a little business with the Fey," Macha said, her voice low and rasping. I couldn't decide if I felt sorry for the Fey. Probably not too sorry.

"And I want to go home. I miss my island," Brigit said. Her voice was soft and warm.

"I'm sorry I kinda broke the world," I said. I spread my hands wide, unsure how to express what I meant. I wasn't that sorry, after all, not when it had ultimately saved us all.

The goddesses laughed.

"You think you are the first?" Macha said.

"There was more than one seal, once," Brigit added. "You are not the only one in history to ever face impossible decisions."

Airmid, Brie, held out her hands to me, and I stepped forward, sliding my clammy fingers into her warm grasp.

"Perhaps a sorcerer stood outside his burning village and swore revenge. Or a girl woke with power in her blood and questions in languages she did not understand. Or perhaps a woman defied the gods and opened a box."

As Brie spoke, her words turned into images, memories that weren't mine but felt a part of me flowing through my vision. A man standing in the heat of a burning building, magic twisting around him as his world died in fire. He reached for what I recognized now as the Pattern, straining to contain more magic than any one body should. That image flowed into a small brown-skinned girl waking alone in a jungle clearing, glowing marks on her skin as she screamed defiance to the skies. Image after image slipped through me: a woman straight off the set of *Rome* reaching for a glowing box, a baby crying as adults turned their back and left them on a stone altar high above a windswept moor.

Brie released my hands and I stepped back, gasping. I took deep breaths and leaned on Alek, trying to regain my mental balance.

"You were not the first," Macha repeated.

"Wow, you really know how to humble a person," I said.

The three laughed again, raven calls and birdsong and summer breezes flowing through their joined voices.

"What are gods for if not to remind mortals of your own insignificance?" Macha said.

With those words, she laughed again. Then she gave me a slight bow, the smallest bend of her neck, before she turned to wings and light, and was gone.

Brigit smiled at me. "Until we meet again, Jade. Alek." She, too, nodded and was gone.

"I suppose I should go clean an oven or something," Brie said with a chuckle.

"I'm glad you are staying," I said. I'd regained my composure and I meant the words. I had changed the world; having a goddess for a neighbor would be comforting in more ways than one. "Is Ciaran?" I hadn't seen him since before the last battle.

"He is, don't worry. You are stuck with us. My baking might even improve without the interference of those two," Brie said. She winked at me and then walked on normal, sneaker-encased feet toward her back door. No magic disappearing act. That, too, was comforting.

"So," I said, looking up at Alek. "That happened." The future was already proving to be interesting. Come what may, I figured having a goddess on my side wouldn't be the worst. At the least maybe I'd score some free cupcakes. No one said an apocalypse had to be all bad.

I lay in bed, unable to sleep. Alek was awake; I could hear it in his breathing.

"Rest, Jade," he murmured.

I curled against him and rested my hand on his chest. Magic sang in my blood, and I felt my dragon beneath my skin aching to stretch her wings.

"I can't. I need to fireball something or fly or I don't know."

"So go fly," Alek said with a soft chuckle.

"That easy, huh?"

"Do you need me to roar for you?" He didn't have to sound so amused.

I hesitated and thought about it. But the dragon was there, part of me now, part of this strange new reality I had forged with my choices.

"No." I sat up. It was dark in our bedroom, but not so dark I couldn't make out the shape of Alek's face and see the glint of his open eyes. "I'll only be a minute or five."

"I love you," Alek said. His fingers brushed my cheek. "All of you."

I swallowed hard against the knot his words put in my throat. "You know how much I love you, right?"

Alek laughed again. "You turned back time to save

me. You ended the world to save me."

I sucked in a surprised breath. I didn't know how he knew that first part. A conversation for another night, another time. "Damn right," I said as I bent to kiss him. "I ended the world for you and nobody else."

Wylde was silent this late at night. Streetlamps glowed and a breeze danced through shadowed branches whispering secrets to the stars. I used magic to lift me onto the roof of my building.

This time shifting to my dragon was as easy as the space between breaths. One moment I was human, small and frail, the next I was dragon, my nose finding scents and my ears catching sounds my other form would never smell nor hear. I spread my wings and soared into the sky. The air grew thinner and colder, a welcome and refreshing change from the heat of the day that still lingered in the cement and stone below.

I spiraled lazily over my town, seemingly alone in the vast sky. Stars winked and danced over and around me as wisps of cloud played with the waning moon. Below me, Wylde sparkled against the dark sea of wilderness stretching out beyond it, a glowing island in the River of No Return.

Below slept everyone I loved. My found family. My

heart. My home. Whatever came next, I would keep my people safe. I sang this to the empty sky, my voice rolling like thunder into the dark.

Folding my wings, I dove for the light.

If you want to be notified when Annie Bellet's next novel or collection is released, please sign up for the mailing list by going to: http://tinyurl.com/anniebellet Your email address will never be shared and you can unsubscribe at any time. Want to find more Twenty-Sided Sorceress books? Go here http://anniebellet.com/series/twenty-sided-sorceress/ for links and more information.

Word-of-mouth and reviews are vital for any author to succeed. If you enjoyed the book, please tell your friends and consider leaving a review wherever you purchased it. Even a few lines sharing your thoughts on this story would be extremely helpful for other readers. Thank you!

Get ready for a brand new series set in the world of the Twenty-Sided Sorceress coming in October, 2020! Follow Alek's sister Kira on her adventures!

Kira solves her problems with a big gun, and she rarely has the same problem twice. *Bad Moon on the Rise* is the first book in the *Six-Gun Shifters* series. Pre-order this exciting new Urban Fantasy now!
https://anniebellet.com/books/bad-moon-on-the-rise/

Also by Annie Bellet

The Gryphonpike Chronicles:
Witch Hunt
Twice Drowned Dragon
A Stone's Throw
Dead of Knight
The Barrows (Omnibus Vol. 1)
Brood Mother
Into the North

Chwedl Duology:
A Heart in Sun and Shadow
The Raven King (Winter 2021)

Pyrrh Considerable Crimes Division Series:
Avarice
Wrath (Fall 2020)

Short Story Collections:
Till Human Voices Wake Us
Dusk and Shiver
Forgotten Tigers and Other Stories

About the Author

Annie Bellet lives and writes in the Netherlands. She is the *USA Today* bestselling author of the *Gryphonpike Chronicles* and the *Twenty-Sided Sorceress* series. Follow her at her website at www.anniebellet.com

Made in the USA
Columbia, SC
03 December 2020